'TIS HER SEASON
A ROYAL REGARD PREQUEL NOVELLA

SAILING HOME
BOOK TWO

MARI A. CHRISTIE

'TIS HER SEASON

Previously published as 'Tis Her Season by Mariana Gabrielle.

Charlotte Amberly would rather eat a lump of coal for Christmas dinner than marry the Marquess of Firthley, so when her parents cancel her London Season in favor of a rush to the altar, the feisty debutante takes husband-hunting into her own hands.

Alexander Marloughe, reluctant heir to a marquessate, would rather not spend his holiday dashing through the snow after a flibberti-gibbet just out of the schoolroom, but no woman before Charlotte has ever led him such a merry chase.

This is a prequel to Royal Regard.

PROLOGUE

Charlotte sat bolt upright in bed. Screams echoed across the frozen grounds to Brittlestep Manor, seemingly all the way from Evercreech. She lit the candle at her bedside, pulled a dressing gown on over her nightrail, grabbed the iron fireplace poker from the hearth, and flew out her bedchamber door and down the hall. By the time she reached the front door, her father's butler was already there with a pistol in his hand. When she nodded, he flung open the door.

"You bloody bitch! Come back here!"

A young woman threw herself through the entryway as if blown by the hard wind that whipped around her into the foyer. Almost falling at Charlotte's feet, she managed to remain standing only by leaning against a wall, bent over, her breathing heavy and coarse, sobs threatening to overwhelm her reason—if they hadn't already.

"Remove yourself from the grounds, Mr. Smithson," the butler intoned, pistol pointed directly at the forehead of the pursuer. "You will not be warned again."

"Go now, Jeremy, or I swear, I will beat you to death myself!" Charlotte yelled, brandishing the poker.

Snarling, slurring his words, stumbling across the graveled drive, the man fell back, barking, "It's not over, you hatchet-faced whore. You can't hide in there forever, and Effingale's not here to stop me. I'll be back for you with the magistrate."

The girl fell against the wall, choked by the same sounds made by animals caught in traps. Holding her arm at the elbow, she slid to a seat on the floor. Wild, red-blonde hair framed a bruised cheek and blackened right eye; her cut and swollen lower lip oozed blood. Terror-filled blue-green eyes squeezed shut when she flinched away from the butler's offered hand—a man she had known since birth, who had never been anything but kind.

"I think he's broken my shoulder, Charlotte. I can't move it."

The butler sighed and sent the night footman to ride for the doctor, no stranger to being called to the Effingales' manor house for this purpose. The housekeeper rushed to help Charlotte support the girl, clucking her tongue.

"Your bedchamber is ready for you, Miss Smithson. And I'll send up some tea." Taking in the thin nightrail hanging on her lanky form, the motherly old woman added, "Haven't eaten a bite since last time you were here, by the look of it, but I don't suppose you'll want a meal with your lip in that state. Perhaps some broth."

Balancing her cousin, Bella, against her shoulder, Charlotte opened the door to the bedchamber adjoining hers, easing her over to the canopied bed while the housekeeper laid a fire in the stone hearth. Carefully settling Bella back into the pillows, listing slightly to the right to accommodate the shoulder, Charlotte sent a maid for hot water, towels, and the medicine box, and told her abigail to find a clean nightrail in Bella's wardrobe.

"Only Jeremy?" Charlotte asked, voice gentler than her countenance.

Bella shook her head, then set her hand on her forehead, as though trying to clear away a mental fog. "No, Father, too. He is the one who hurt my arm, but he is floored now. They were drinking."

"Are they not always drinking?" Charlotte snapped. "And John, I presume?"

"No, he is in London." Bella's tears fell faster. "I wish it were John. He isn't so..."

Charlotte patted Bella in the hand. "I know. Though 'not such a monster' is hardly a recommendation. Can you remove the nightrail over your shoulder?"

Cradling the elbow, Bella shook her head, so Charlotte cut the bloodstained linen off her cousin's body with scissors, then draped the dressing gown over her shoulders, arranging it in a semblance of modesty, covering it further with the quilt. "Perhaps one good thing will come of this."

Bella's laugh cut into Charlotte's gut.

"I'm quite serious." Charlotte had never seen Bella so disheartened, even on countless other nights like this. "Father will never allow you back there if Uncle Jasper has broken your arm, no matter what Mother says."

CHAPTER ONE

December 15, 1803
Somerset, England

The snow falling outside the frosted drawing room window blanketed Charlotte Amberly's mood as surely as it did the garden on which she gazed. Usually, she loved the Yuletide season, but she could hardly keep her mind on wassail and holly berries, knowing who would be staying at least through Twelfth Night, assuredly planning to meet her under the kissing bough.

The Marquess of Firthley, Charlotte's new betrothed, was expected in a few days for an indefinite stay, and if Charlotte's mother had her way, he wouldn't leave until they were married. When a viscount's daughter snared a marquess, it behooved her to leg-shackle him before he could run.

"Lord Firthley's note said he was bringing his grandson." Minerva Amberly, Lady Effingale, calmly stitched the outline of a Christmas rose on an altar cloth intended as a gift for the vicar's wife.

"Yes, Mother. You've told me twenty times. I must be kind to the poor, motherless child, so the marquess will believe me a good grandmother for his heir."

"Quite right, and you needn't take that tone."

"I will be a grandmother before I am eighteen," she grumbled.

"Better than a spinster before you are twenty."

"I've not even met him!" she argued, going so far as to stomp her foot.

Lady Effingale would brook no such nonsense from a recalcitrant daughter. "Then it is fortunate he wants you sight unseen."

Between the flare of her mother's nostrils and the arch of her left eyebrow, Charlotte's rebellion fizzled—briefly.

"He wants Papa's voting bloc, not me," Charlotte protested under her breath, but before her mother could castigate her again, she moaned, "I was to make my curtsey next month! How can you just ignore an invitation from the queen?"

"One of your husband's relations will present you at Court as his marchioness. He has the king's ear, you know."

Dropping onto the window seat, hiding her grimace behind the curtain, Charlotte muttered, "Yes, Mother. You've said."

Lady Effingale set down her needlework to sort through her basket of silks, finally finding a length of dark green. "You should be grateful to be the wife of a man of considerable fortune and influence."

"Yes, Mother."

The sounds of running and yelling down the hall came rapidly closer until Charlotte's two younger brothers dashed into the room, throwing a rounders ball between them. The ball promptly slammed into the teapot and sent it flying off the table next to Charlotte, into the skirts of her new pale pink dress, leaving a huge brown stain. Guy and Hugh, ages twelve and fourteen respectively, stopped short at their mother's screeching and Charlotte's rage.

"You hellions! Get out! Get back to the nursery before I break you into pieces and return you to Eton in a box!"

Although she had complained endlessly to her mother and Bella about the wishy-washy color of the gown, it was not improved by being soiled. And she was in a far worse temper now than she had been a week ago.

Guy scurried to retrieve the ball, while Hugh drew himself up into a dignified and offended stance worthy of the viscount he would one day become.

"We no longer reside in the nursery, and you have no call to screech. I heard Mother tell you just this morning, you 'must improve your sense of decorum.'"

By contrast to his brother's false indignity, Guy's sheepish smile apologized for the teapot, the yelling, and Charlotte's dress, though he was not contrite enough for their mother.

"But for her execrable language, your sister is quite right," she snapped. "Where is Isabella? She was to be keeping watch over you, was she not?"

Now Hugh looked a bit chary. "Er, she is... was... uh... detained. And we are too old for a governess, at any rate." He straightened his shoulders. "We are both Eton men now. Papa said so."

Charlotte strode toward him, and he fell back. "Little Eton boys, rather. Go let Bella out of whatever closet you've locked her into, or I will shut you up in the nursery on bread and water and give your Christmas gifts to the children in the poorhouse!"

Both boys ran out of the room, still throwing the ball between them, gaining more volume once they cleared the door. Lady Effingale took up her embroidery again, remarking, "You will wish to be gentler with the marquess's grandson."

Charlotte dabbed at her dress with a table napkin, but the exercise was hopeless. The stain reached from waist to hem and crossed the dress from side to side. She dropped the napkin on the tea tray, waved her hand toward the door, and turned up her nose.

"No sane woman will ever want to marry either of them. You will be stuck with them your entire life."

"I'm sure that is not true," her mother said. However, her lips quivered just slightly when she added, "They are both growing up too handsome for any girl's good, and Hugh will be Effingale one day. Surely some woman will suffer him, if only for his title and lands. I do agree, though, his brother may ever be a bachelor, and probably an incorrigible rake." Dropping the altar cloth in her lap, peering through her lorgnette at her daughter's dress, she added, "You'd better go find Isabella, so that she can help you change your dress and try to remove the stain."

Yes, Charlotte thought, *Bella is sure to be more sympathetic.*

CHAPTER TWO

Three days later...

"Ouch! Must you?"

Bella apologized for pulling too hard at a knot in Charlotte's hair, and Charlotte's regret for snapping was extracted from her mouth almost as painfully. "My apologies. It's only—"

"The marquess will finally be here tomorrow, and you wish he would not."

Charlotte sighed. "I don't understand how Papa can do this to me. He has always stood up to Mother before." Rather than passing it over her shoulder, she threw a diamond hair comb on the vanity table, as though the jewels were tin. "Politics! It is all politics. I wish there had never been a House of Lords. And I wish Papa had never set aside a dowry. I would be better off as a seamstress."

Bella reached across for the comb, carefully placing it in Charlotte's lush black hair, holding the high curls in place on the left side, level with the right. "You would be an awful seamstress. You cannot sew a straight line."

"You take my meaning, Bella. And stop smirking. You would be in a poor temper, too, if your father planned to marry you off to some old man."

"My father would marry me off to a hundred-year-old drunken wife-beater in debtors' prison, if there were advantage in it." Bella's tone stopped just short of complaint.

Ignoring that appalling truth, Charlotte continued, "He probably has slobbery lips. And spots on his hands." She shuddered. At seventeen, spittle and discolored skin seemed the worst fates imaginable, until another thought occurred. "Oh, no..." Her eyes widened.

"What is it?" Bella asked, looking over the coiffure again, silver hairbrush hovering.

"He will want to bed me."

"Charlotte!" Bella turned an extraordinary shade of crimson, cheeks all but throbbing.

"He will! Nettie says it can be quite nice if the gentleman is kind, but I will never know now, will I? Some ugly, fat, old man with dry, papery lips and skin like crumpled parchment? It will be awful." Yanking the hairbrush from Bella's hand, she threw it across the room, where it shattered a vase. Bella groaned. So did Charlotte. Her mother would now feel it her duty to check on them, and Charlotte was not nearly prepared to be inspected.

Sure enough, the door crashed against the wall when Lady Effingale rushed in. Bella was already on her knees, gathering pieces of china in a pouch she made of her dingy, gray skirt.

"What is it? Is everyone unharmed?"

"Yes, Mother. I simply knocked a vase from the shelf."

Narrowed eyes taking in the hairbrush on the floor, lips pressed into a thin line, her mother warned in the low tone usually reserved for Charlotte's brothers, "You will do nothing to ruin this arrangement, Charlotte Amberly. Not one thing."

Bella backed into a corner.

"You will be happy and charming and sweet to the marquess and the little boy and act as though you wish nothing more than his honorable attentions, or I will make you regret it. Do you hear me? This marriage is of great importance to your father, and you will not destroy the agreement with your willful, unruly tantrums, or believe you me, I will use that hairbrush on you in a manner inconsistent with its purpose."

Willful, unruly tantrums threatening, Charlotte growled, "Yes, Mother. Of course, Mother. Anything you wish, *Mother*."

CHAPTER THREE

The next day...

Snow piled up outside the door, falling heavier and heavier as the day wore on. Charlotte had never seen so much snow in December; it was almost as if the Almighty Himself were taking her part in the ongoing quarrel with her parents. She hoped the marquess's carriage would be delayed again, perhaps lose a wheel, or be stuck in a ditch or a snowdrift. Perhaps, if she were lucky, the old man would freeze to death and leave her alone. She corrected herself for such spiteful thoughts, but couldn't quite hold in a sigh. Her life would be much happier if no Marquess of Firthley existed.

She had been looking forward to her come-out as long as she could remember. While other girls giggled and planned for a wedding, she had planned for ballrooms and beaux, and her curtsey to the queen. The queen had been her entire reason for learning to curtsey, after her nurse told stories about girls being presented and going on to marry handsome gentlemen with titles and plenty of money. The perfection of her Town manners was entirely due to her plans for her Season.

She had known since age six what color dresses she wanted—sea-foam green to match her eyes; which jewels she would wear from her mother's collection—the emeralds to accent her dress; the types of decorations she would insist upon—an ocean of flowers, all white; and the ladies and gentlemen she would invite—everyone who was anyone. She had collected recipes for years for the food that would be served at *her* ball. She should have been traveling to London in a matter of days to finally have *her* Season.

No matter how many other girls might be presented, Charlotte would be the prettiest of them. A diamond of the first water. An Incomparable. She would make the most impressive and important match in history, barring only the Royal family. She might even land a prince, if one happened to be seeking a bride.

Instead, by the time she would have boarded her father's carriage for Town, she would be shackled to an ancient marquess who wanted her dowry, and whose good opinion her father wished to cultivate. She had never considered she might ever be so unlucky.

A loud banging on the front door interrupted her dismal woolgathering, and she slipped her feet into the brocaded shoes that *didn't* match the dress that *wasn't* the printed silk dinner gown her mother had chosen. Charlotte had changed her attire four times today. First, her very finest morning gown, then a promenade dress, then a tea gown, with changes in accessories and coiffure each time, waiting endlessly for her future husband to appear. Now, finally, a dinner dress—of her own choosing—that made her look fat and sallow, the quilted nankeen twill sturdy enough to withstand his grandson, surely a horrid little boy who would tear the seams and vomit on whatever she wore, just to be nasty.

Pulling a Prussian-blue-and-blush-pink Kashmir shawl about

her shoulders, she dragged her feet down the hall from the library, where she had been watching the candles burn low, hoping for one more day's reprieve. Freezing cold air blew in the front entrance and up the stairs before the heavy oak door was closed, and she shivered under her wrap.

Not even one more night to pretend she would remain free.

"Of course, Your Lordship," she heard faintly, "Lord and Lady Effingale are in the drawing room. They are expecting you. If you will follow me." The Effingale's butler, Latham, gave her no quarter, either, rapidly showing the man in to see her parents before she could get a good look at him through the pine garland wrapping the first-floor banister.

Before long, someone would come to collect her for this wretched meeting with the awful man who was to be her husband. Better she should jump out her bedroom window and escape before she was summoned. She turned to do just that when she heard a footman open the front door once more. Over her shoulder, she saw a man stomp his boots on the stone floor. She turned and watched him shake the snow off his greatcoat before handing it, and his top hat, to the footman, who was struggling not to laugh aloud at something indiscernible. Charlotte had never before seen a gentleman joke with a footman, and rather hoped Latham didn't catch him at it.

He was a young man, though older than she, and handsome, with dark-brown hair, tanned skin, and an easy smile. When he was escorted down the hall to the drawing room, Charlotte found herself not quite so inclined to throw herself from the window. Rather than wait to discover her fate or induce it herself, she squared her shoulders and took the stairs as through she were descending into the ballroom at Carlton House.

At the drawing room door, she waited, hoping to hear anything that might be to her advantage, but the voices were too low. When Latham cleared his throat behind her, she jumped.

Without any acknowledgment she had been eavesdropping, she held her head high and opened the door.

"My dear," her father said, all smiles, crossing the room. "Come in, come in."

Her mother's mouth fell open then snapped shut at the sight of her daughter's attire, her eyebrows flying up to meet her hairline, and Charlotte bit her lip to keep from smirking. She held her head just a bit straighter and adjusted the shawl over the shoulders of the high-necked gown, knowing she would pay for her insurrection, probably for days to come.

Thankfully, Papa wouldn't know a good gown from a bad one; she was his beautiful baby girl, no matter what she wore. "Lord Firthley, might I present my daughter, Charlotte Amberly?"

The slightest bit miffed that her father held this gentleman in higher regard than he did his own daughter, presenting her as though she were a child, not a young lady ready to be married, she hid her pique behind a fake smile, curtseying as low as she might in the Queen's Drawing Room.

"My lord," she said, peeking from under her lashes. He was tall, not undignified, but her worst fears were realized: his skin looked like translucent oilskin, his hair was so thin and colorless, he might as well have none, and dark spots showed on his balding pate. The hand held out to take hers was as gangly as he was, long fingers bony and weak, like the wing of a dying sparrow fluttering between her fingers.

"My dear Miss Amberly, I am delighted to make your acquaintance." He looked her up and down as she rose, as though she was a horse for sale at Tattersall's, lingering on the foot-long Turkey red fringe of the shawl. She flipped it across her forearm as she looked for the little boy, but only caught the amused eyes of the other gentleman, who had risen from a chair when she entered, but remained across the room, making no effort to interrupt. She wished he would. She wished anyone would.

"Miss Amberly, may I present my grandson, Alexander Marloughe, Earl of Herrendon?" Even as he made the introduction, the marquess stared at her bosom as though it were framed by the almost-indecent gown her mother had chosen.

She looked around again for a horrid little spoiled brat peeking out from behind a chair. The earl smiled at the gasp she gracelessly swallowed when he bent over her hand. Up close, he was as handsome as she had thought. His hair was sandy, lightened by proximity to his face, darker than most Englishman, but not enough so to make him look foreign. His nose was straight, his teeth even and bright behind a grin that seemed to embrace all the joy she had ever felt. Once drawn into the ambit of his smile, his luminous eyes and a sardonically arched brow held her there.

"As you are peering about the room at a height of two feet, I gather you were expecting someone younger?"

"Ye—I mean no, my lord." She felt herself blushing and, not for the first time, wished she weren't so fair. "Of course n—only, we were—I was—I only thought..."

Her mother's eyes flashed, and her head shook just slightly.

Charlotte choked out, "Welcome to our home, my lords. Has Mother rung for tea? Surely you must be chilled through."

The earl raised a brandy glass, and Lady Effingale smiled at Charlotte's gracious affability, eyes only slightly narrowed, looking closely for fault. "Tea will be here shortly. Please, gentlemen, take a seat."

Charlotte slid into a chair as fast as she could, to avoid being seated on a sofa, and forced into close proximity with her future husband, but the decrepit old man took a seat in the nearest armchair. The earl, by contrast, sat as far away as he could while still maintaining a semblance of manners. Ankle crossed over his knee, arm draped across the arm of a chair turned slightly away from the assemblage, Lord Herrendon took in the art on the walls, sipping the brandy, distancing himself from the conversation.

Perhaps, she thought, spirits rising just slightly, she wasn't meant to marry the old man at all! Perhaps the betrothal would be to this handsome, young man now staring into the fireplace. Trying not to slip sidelong glances at him, and wondering what made him look so sad, she warmed to her line of reasoning. Men never wanted to be married. Surely his reticence could be chalked up to—

"It must be very strange, Miss Amberly, to be affianced without once meeting me," the marquess began, his tongue wetting his lower lip as he stared as her chest.

Her spirits dropped like a ship's anchor.

She cleared her throat, pulling the shawl tighter, feeling as though she were naked under his heated gaze. "It is, my lord, a bit. But of course..." She could barely free the words from her gritted teeth. "I will do as my father bids. I trust he has my best interest in mind."

A soft snort from across the room was ignored by everyone but Charlotte, who wanted, alternately, to giggle at the earl and defend her father from this interloper. Before she could do either, the marquess presented her with a square, shallow, velvet box she would treat like a snake, were her parents not watching. She stretched out her hand to take it, moving swiftly to keep him from touching her fingers. It must be a parure, and a sizable one, given the dimensions and weight of the box.

"The Firthley rubies, of course, will be in your keeping. You may consider them a Christmas gift."

She unhooked the latch and opened the box, hardly wanting to look. Rubies the size of blackbird eggs, set in a rose-tinted gold. Beautiful. Stunning. A necklace that reached to the collarbone, bracelets, hair clips, a tiara, and a ring.

A ring.

The marquess placed the heavy, icy gold on her finger. Everyone in the room beamed except Charlotte, but when she looked away from all of the smiling, she noticed the earl wore a frown, too.

There were not enough rubies in the world to make her marry the Marquess of Firthley.

A few minutes too late to interrupt her unwelcome betrothal, a maid appeared with the tea trolley, and Charlotte was tasked by her mother to pour.

The earl kept his seat, blatantly turning the chair farther away, picking up a newspaper her father must have left on the table nearest the fireplace. Before Charlotte finished handing around teacups, Lord Herrendon's head was hidden behind the newssheets.

"Might I offer you a slice of plum cake, Lord Herrendon? Or gingerbread?" Charlotte attempted. "Our cook is known for her light hand with a batter." She held out a delicate china plate rimmed with gold, but the earl acted as though she hadn't even spoken.

His grandfather snapped, "Herrendon, I beg you mind your manners, Sir!"

Lord Herrendon poked his head over the top of the pages and shrugged. "I have nothing to add to the discussion, I'm afraid." His face disappeared again, and he rattled the pages.

A loud sigh left Lord Firthley's flaring nostrils before he turned back. "I apologize for my grandson's poor conduct. He was raised by his mother's parents in Greece, and they were..." he whispered, "...shopkeepers."

Charlotte's mother gasped, her father coughed, and the man behind the newspaper reacted not at all, but to say, "My mother's father owned the largest shipping concern in the southern part of Europe before Napoleon developed too much ambition, and I own what is left of it now. No one in my family has ever seen the back room of a shop."

As though he hadn't spoken, his grandfather continued, "He

is, however, my heir, so I am hopeful," he raised his voice as though the man five feet away were hard of hearing, "the young man might yet be taught to behave in company."

"I know perfectly well how to behave in company," said the disembodied voice behind the newspaper. "I simply find myself superfluous to discussion of your marriage to a girl not even out yet and young enough to be my sister." He rattled the pages again and folded them. "A much-younger sister." Standing and stretching his arms behind his back, he added, "Perhaps, Lord Effingale, you have a library to which I might retire until your *business transaction* is concluded?"

Lady Effingale stood immediately, face flaming, and offered, "I can show you to the rooms we've set aside."

"Excellent. A bath and a change of clothes will be just the thing. I expect my valet will be waiting." He bowed in a way that was both disrespectful and entirely proper. "My lords, Miss Amberly, presumably, as it is so late in the evening, I will see you on the morrow."

CHAPTER FOUR

Christmas night, 1803

Charlotte loitered in the dark hall outside her brother's room, candlestick in hand, pelisse buttoned tightly over her riding habit. When she heard no noise behind the door, she cleared her throat. Nothing. She shuffled her feet. Still nothing. She thumped her shoulder against the wall just loudly enough to call attention to herself inside the room, but only to wake one brother, not both.

She shuffled her feet again and picked up the bag she had packed with a few changes of clothing, a hairbrush, and what was left of last week's pin money, after she had bought the hideous pink-and-blue shawl. If she had to shuffle much more, her slippers would wear through.

"What is it? Who is there?" Hugh's squeaking voice sounded under the door. Perfect. He was afraid, as he always was when he woke in a darkened room. She had snuck in half an hour ago to blow out the covered candle he always left burning. Her brother threw open the door, a four-branch candelabra lighting up the hall.

Charlotte gasped as though she were actually startled. "Hugh! What are you doing awake?"

He eyed her clothes and drawled, "I could ask the same thing. Where are you going in the middle of the night?"

"Er... nowhere... special..."

He drew himself up in the pose he effected when he wished to pretend he was already the viscount. "I can see you are lying, Sister. Will you tell me, or will I wake Mother and Father right now?"

Her face blanched. "No!" she whispered, pushing him into the bedchamber. "No, don't do that. I'll... I'll give you..." She reached into her reticule and removed a few notes. "I'll give you five guineas."

The execution of her plan was worth a hundred times that—if she had so much ready coin. She would beg, borrow, or steal after four days of taking sleigh rides with the marquess, playing dinner companion to the marquess, learning piquet from the marquess, going to the village with the marquess. If the word 'marquess' left her mother's mouth one more time, Charlotte would scream. Earlier this evening, he had given her his former wife's wedding veil as a Christmas present, quite the most ghoulish gift she had ever received, along with more jewels; this time, a pearl choker, which made her feel like a rabid pet. A few minutes later, she had wished she could bite the man.

Tomorrow night, her father had said, when the Effingales hosted the neighboring gentry for a Boxing Day supper, her betrothal would be announced publicly, with a wedding soon to follow.

Hugh held out his hand and put the money into the pocket of his banyan. "Where are you going?"

"I'm... You cannot tell anyone... Do you hear me? You cannot tell a living soul. I've paid you five guineas for your silence. Do you promise?"

"I suppose," he drawled.

"I've met a soldier... in the village... I cannot marry that ghastly old man, so I... or rather, we... we are..."

His eyes rounded. "Never say you are eloping?"

Charlotte didn't say it.

"On Christmas?"

She shrugged.

"Mother will lose her mind! Father, too. They will murder you!"

"Not if you say nothing. I have to go. We have to be in Ports—Bristol by tomorrow evening."

"Portsmouth, eh?"

"I said Bristol!"

"Yes. Bristol. Of course. How silly of me to think you might lie while you are running away into the night." He was quiet for a moment, then said, "Ten guineas, and I will say nothing about Portsmouth until morning."

"I suppose it will have to do." She reached into the reticule and handed him two more notes and three coins. "You greedy devil."

"You had better use the head start, before I send Father after you." With the slightest bit of concern, far more than usual, he said, "If you do this, it will be the end of you."

"It will be nothing of the sort. Just do your part and leave the rest to me."

He gestured for her to leave his room. When the door closed behind her, she let out her nervous breath, resting her back against the wall. He would decide it was his duty to wake their parents before the sun came up, but not much more, which gave her less than five hours to stay ahead.

Sneaking into the stables proved difficult with the bitter cold wind whipping around her. The light of her candle extinguished itself not two steps outside the kitchen door, so she fought her way through the dark and the snow, now calf-high. She should never be taking her mare out in such conditions, but Lord Firthley had brought a special license with him from London, and the vicar would be attending tomorrow evening's festivities. She tightened the strings of her bonnet and wished she had brought a shawl as well as her pelisse, but there was no turning back. If she didn't leave now, she would be married by the end of the week.

Courage, she told herself. *Nothing is ever accomplished by courting safety*. If she wanted safety, she would marry the rich, old codger sleeping down the hall from her parents.

Setting her bag down just inside the stable door, she moved rapidly and silently to the stall where her mare, Aurelia, was kept. "Shh, my sweet. I know it is cold, but we must be off to Bristol..." She kept up a quiet monologue while she saddled the horse, and turned to lead Aurie into the larger stable.

"Name of Heaven!" she shrieked when she bumped into Lord Herrendon, who had been lounging against the wall, just out of her sight. "What are you doing here?" she hissed.

"Returning from a jaunt into your lovely village."

"That is evident by the smell of ale on your breath."

"Then why did you ask?" he smirked. "The real question, Miss Amberly, is what *you* are doing here. Proper young ladies are abed this time of night, not saddling horses and preparing to travel to Bristol. Especially on Christmas."

"It is no longer Christmas."

"I concede," he said, after a glance at his pocket watch. "Boxing Day, then."

"How did you... you have been eavesdropping! How long have you been there?"

"Long enough to know your horse settles when you sing *Orange in Bloom*."

"You beast! You horrible man! Go back into the house right now, and pretend you have seen nothing."

"Really, what kind of a gentleman would I be if I did that?"

"Clearly, you are no kind of gentleman, or you would have made your presence known."

He shrugged. "As I have not, however, and am now in possession of a goodly portion of your plan, you must know I cannot allow you to take this course. I may be no one's vision of a gentleman, but nonetheless, I cannot allow a gently-bred young lady to ride across country through a blizzard by herself."

She stuck her chin out. "How do you plan to stop me?"

He reached out and took the horse's bridle. No matter how Aurie tossed her head or whinnied, he kept hold, and the more Charlotte fought Lord Herrendon, the more Aurie spooked, until she nearly bolted, held back only by his hold on the reins. "Stop that! Someone will hear!"

"Indeed."

With his other hand, he risked his fingers to reach up and pet the horse's nose, humming *Orange in Bloom* until she quieted.

"Have you brought food?" The corner of his lip turned up just slightly when Aurie nickered in his ear.

"For what?"

He stared, all trace of amusement wiped clean. "To eat."

"I have ten guineas," she said, nose in the air. "I will buy food."

"Along the road?" The smug look reappeared. "The icy, cold, abandoned road?"

Her voice wavered just slightly. "That's right."

"And for Aurie? Were you planning to bring oats for her? There will be no forage in the middle of winter, you understand." His lips twitched.

Charlotte looked around, as though a bag of oats might present itself.

Lord Herrendon kept stroking the horse's head, scratching behind her ears. "And what if you and Aurie are stranded in the snow between villages?"

"That will not happen."

"No?" He reached out to rub the sleeve of her pelisse between his fingers. "Have you brought a thicker coat? You'll catch your death."

"I will be perfectly fine!" she growled, dragging her coat away. "I am a viscount's daughter. Give me my horse."

"I will strike you a bargain, Miss Amberly."

She turned a cold shoulder, though she wasn't sure it could be any colder than it already was under the autumn pelisse. "Striking bargains is vulgar."

"So is leaving your house without telling your parents in the middle of the night."

She grabbed for the bridle, but he shifted to keep her out of arm's reach. Arching one brow, he said, "Will you strike an *agreement*, then?"

"I suppose you want my virtue?"

He laughed aloud. "No. No, I don't want your virtue." He looked her up and down. "Such as it is. You are set on this course, presumably, as you would prefer not to marry my grandfather, who must be at least four times your age, and as it happens, I sympathize."

"And you don't like your grandfather," she guessed.

"Quite. So I will offer you this. I cannot allow you to travel to Bristol alone." He held up his hand to stop her objections. "You will, therefore, travel in my carriage, as civilized people ought, and in return, you will agree not to act like a spoilt child all the way there."

"My reputation will be—"

"Ruined? My dear, you are already utterly compromised. Were it not for the fact I have no desire to marry, I would have your dowry in hand this minute. Another reason I will not allow you to travel alone. I, at least, do not have improper designs on you, but I cannot say that will be the case for every man you might meet along the road. In fact," he said, his eyes once again roaming from the tip of her bonnet to the toes of her half-boots, "I can rather warrant the opposite."

Reaching for her horse again, she instead came up against his hard chest, and his free hand grasped hers. "Ah, ah, Miss Amberly. If you go around touching men, your reputation will be in tatters without my help."

The fire in her cheeks could almost warm her, and she wrenched her hand out of his. "Are you not concerned you'll have to marry me if we're caught?"

"No, that is not a concern at all." When she preened, he added, "I would simply refuse. I care not a whit for Society's good opinion, nor your father's, and I would lay good odds I am better with a pistol."

Her mouth opened and closed, indignation naught but a squeak in her throat. While she wasn't expressing her ire, he efficiently stripped Aurelia of her tack and put her back in her stall. Taking Charlotte by her arm, his other hand at the small of her back, he guided her, not entirely ungently, toward the coach and said, "You may as well stay warm while I hook up the cattle." He handed her his greatcoat. "And put this on. You are an idiot, running about in a pelisse and silk gloves in weather like this."

"You'll—"

"Believe me, I will take it back before I climb up to drive. Get. In. The. Coach. Or I call for your father right now."

She scrambled inside.

CHAPTER FIVE

December 26, 1803
Somerset, England

"She has done what?!"

Aunt Minerva's voice might have punctured Bella's eardrum if she had been standing much closer. As it was, she was too close for comfort, an arm's reach away from Bella's weak shoulder. Neither her aunt nor uncle had ever laid a hand on her, but just the thought of being touched in anger had her sinking into the wallpaper.

When Hugh had woken his parents with the news before dawn, Aunt Minerva had come looking for Bella, pulling her from the bed, subjecting her to a tirade before Bella could even find a dressing gown.

"S-She's..." Bella stuttered, "Perhaps she's... I mean... maybe she left a note..." Of course Charlotte had left a message, but she had made Bella swear she wouldn't point out the folded parchment on her dressing table until morning.

Pushing through the door that connected the two girls' bedchambers, Bella slunk to the vanity and pretended to be searching through the crystalline jars for what she already knew was there. She slipped the letter out from underneath the stacked jewel boxes Charlotte had been given by the marquess. In her cousin's typically dramatic fashion, the ruby ring sat atop the pile.

"It appears she's left this."

Grabbing at the note and ruby ring in a way that betrayed her ignoble origins, Lady Effingale shrieked when she read the few lines.

Forgive me, but I have met a soldier, and I know you would never deny our love. By now, I am on my way to Portsmouth to board a ship to Scotland. Wish me happy. I will write as soon as I can.

"A soldier?! A soldier?! Good God, what is she thinking? She's ruined! Utterly ruined!"

"Perhaps not a soldier," Uncle Howard intoned in a dark voice from the doorway. "Herrendon's carriage is gone. The stable master heard noises in the night, but when the earl left for the village, he told the grooms not to bother waking when he returned, that he would take care of his own mount."

Aunt Minerva pulled her husband into the room and shut the door. "The marquess might cry off if he thinks she's been compromised. If his own flesh and blood has done it, so much the worse." She prodded at her husband's arm, moaning, "Whatever will we do, Effingale?"

He turned his shoulder against his wife and approached Bella tentatively, as though she were a cat who might bolt or bite. Bella sank farther into the corner, trying to make herself smaller than a kitten, smaller than a mouse. Small enough no one in her family would ever lay eyes in her again.

"What can you tell me, my dear? Did Charlotte tell you nothing?"

Bella shook her head, words stuck in her throat.

"Of course our hoyden of a daughter told her something! They are thick as thieves. If you don't tell me everything you know, you wretched girl, I will send you back to my brother before the day is out and tell him to beat you bloody! Do you understand me?"

At Bella's squeak, Uncle Howard pointed to the door. "Out, Lady Effingale. Out!" When she showed no sign of leaving, he took her by the upper arm and physically removed her to the hall, then locked the door behind her. They were safe enough from any banging on the door, as she would do anything to keep the marquess from learning about his fiancée's treachery.

He gently led Bella to the bench in front of the vanity and sat her down. Crouching in front of her, he pushed the hair away from her face that had fallen from her braid. "Did Charlotte say anything, sweetling? Anything that might help us find her?"

Bella swallowed and shook her head, but her hesitation must have shown, because her uncle leaned forward and searched her face.

"You understand she could be in awful danger, and not just from her soldier?"

Bella looked away.

"Anything she might have said could help me. Please trust I won't let you or Charlotte come to harm."

Bella nodded, and at this reminder of the gentle nature of the one man in her family who would never maltreat her, she whispered, "She said to say Portsmouth, which likely means Bristol."

"Is it Scotland she intends?"

"I... I don't know, Uncle Howard. She said so, but she's never mentioned a soldier until last night... and she gave me no name. I don't know what she has planned. She was so..."

"So...?"

"So *different*. She was... determined. I mean, she is always stubborn, but never so... resolute... She looked just like Aunt Minerva. And she demanded I say nothing until morning. I couldn't just... You know how she... I mean..." She sniffled. "I'm so sorry, Uncle Howard."

He patted her knee, his eyes ten years older. "I know, Bella, dearest. We Amberlys do put you in the worst predicaments, do we not?"

When the tears welled up, he wiped one away with his thumb, then stood. "You will stay in your room with the door locked until I return. As I am the only one with a key, you should be safe from your aunt's temper."

This was not the first time her uncle had locked her away for her own safety. "Yes, Sir."

"I will tell Latham your father and brothers may not enter the house, and I'll send someone up with a tray."

"Thank you, Uncle Howard."

He pointed to the connecting door, and she scurried through it.

"Yes, I will bring Charlotte back posthaste, Lady Effingale," Bella heard from her position at the connecting door to Charlotte's bedroom. Her aunt and uncle had retired there to discuss their plan, if one could call it a plan—incoherent as it was. However, they remained unaware the two girls had picked a hole near the bottom of the door by the time they were ten, so they could talk back and forth while punished in their separate rooms.

"No, I will not let her talk me around," he continued wearily, "nor allow her some boon for her disobedience." Uncle Howard's putting-his-foot-down voice finally slammed against the door.

"No, you will not be coming with me! It is too cold, and I will travel rough."

Finally, Aunt Minerva stopped mumbling and became strident. "You make certain she understands exactly what I will do to her if ever she should attempt such a thing again. And shoot that soldier—if there is a soldier—on sight. But make sure you put your hands on the marriage lines—if she's been married. Oh, dear Heavens, what will we do if she's run away with a soldier and not even been married? She is a viscount's daughter!" Aunt Minerva's voice gained pitch and speed. "There should be a law against viscount's daughters marrying beneath them! I insist you draft legislation!"

"Lady Effingale, you will please remove yourself from my path so I may be on my way to find our daugh..." His voice trailed off at the sound of a knock.

"Lord and Lady Effingale? I heard raised voices on my way to break my fast. Is there some problem with which I might offer assistance?"

Bella gasped along with both her aunt and uncle. No one would be well served by the marquess finding out his fiancée had decamped, with the possible exception of Charlotte. Even she would be worse off if the marquess put it out in the *ton* she had run away in the middle of the night. She would be better off considered a flirt or a jilt.

"Everything is just fine, Lord Firthley," Aunt Minerva's singsong tone was a warning flag only to someone who had known her for years. "Charlotte is just... poorly this morning, I'm afraid. There will be a meal waiting downstairs."

"Just so," Lord Firthley replied, volume rising slightly to be heard through the door. "Miss Amberly, I do hope you feel better so we may walk in the portrait gallery this afternoon."

"I'm sure she will be feeling fine by then, Lord Firthley. Do have one of the footmen show you to the dining room."

Bella didn't know how Aunt Minerva would manage to produce a no-longer-sick daughter for a walk in the gallery in a few hours' time, but it was not outside the realm of possibility she would dress Bella up in Charlotte's clothes and a veil. Nothing would keep her from marrying her daughter to a marquess, short of death. Or a soldier in Gretna Green.

Once her aunt and uncle had abandoned the room next to hers—he to take a carriage to Gretna Green via Bristol and she to entertain Lord Firthley so thoroughly he would not ask about Charlotte's manufactured illness—Bella took up *The Romance of the Forest,* which Charlotte had finished last week. They were supposed to discuss it together when she finished reading it, but now, if Charlotte were found, she might not be discussing anything with anyone for a very long time. Her mother might lock her in a dungeon, if there were one below the house. And who knew what Lord Firthley might do if she somehow ended up as his wife? No one knew his temperament well enough to say.

Four pages along in the book, a scream pierced her door.

As she rushed down the front stairs toward the dining room, the screaming did not cease. She could hear Latham trying to calm her aunt.

"Your Ladyship, please. If I might escort you to the drawing room, I can have the—"

He looked up when Bella skated into the room, not even trying to hide the fact she had been running.

One glance took in the scene: Lord Firthley, motionless, face down in his eggs; her aunt waving both hands in the air, chair fallen to the floor, opening and closing her eyes as though blinking might wake the marquess; Latham attempting to gather Lady Effingale's hands without restraining her outright, while trying not to be struck by a flying fist.

"Is he...?" Bella asked. Latham nodded, which increased the volume of Aunt Minerva's shrieking.

"Aunt Minerva, please!" Bella clapped her hands together before her aunt's face, which stopped the voluminous noise long enough for Bella to take her elbow. "Please, come with me into the drawing room, and Latham will bring tea."

Perhaps a sign of her bewilderment, Lady Effingale followed along without argument or incident, dazed as a little girl fallen from a horse. Once in the drawing room, Bella poured her aunt a glass of brandy and forced her to sip it.

Aunt Minerva thumped the half-drunk glass of liquor onto the side table and groaned. "She's ruined us, Bella. Charlotte has ruined the entire family."

"I know she has been... hasty... but we will find her, and Lord Firthley's death can hardly be lain at her feet when she is not even in the house."

"I knew she would engulf us in scandal. She has been a headstrong, willful child since she was in leading strings. I should have beaten it out of her long since."

Bella shivered.

"She should be a marchioness right now, not the runaway bride of some soldier. He probably isn't even an officer. She would have been presented to the king, Bella, *the king!*"

"Yes, Aunt Minerva. I know." She patted her aunt's hand and placed the brandy glass back between her fingers. "Drink this. I will go consult with Latham about the bo... Lord Fir... about the situation."

"He cannot be found here, Bella. You cannot allow him to be found in our house, not even our county, if it can be helped. Tell Latham to make arrangements with the coroner. And we must cancel the supper... send footmen with our excuses. We will just have to say..." Her shoulders slumped. "We will have to say something. Charlotte will never make a match if her affianced has fallen dead in her parents' dining room."

Bella shook her head at her aunt's supreme inconsistency, but decided not to point out Charlotte might already be married. Even if she weren't, no doubt she would gleefully celebrate news of the marquess' demise in as inappropriate a manner as she could manage.

CHAPTER SIX

December 26, 1803
The road to Bristol

This was the most miserable plan he had ever made. Well, to be fair, he hadn't made it, but neither had the flibberti-gibbet riding warm and comfortable in his coach while he was frozen solid holding the ribbons. If he hadn't drunk so much, or if he had taken the serving wench up on her offer, or if he had walked away when he saw the very pretty, very young daughter of the house sneaking into the stables at midnight, this would not be such a muddle.

She was a beautiful girl, who would turn heads in any court in Europe with that rich, black hair and pale skin soft as eiderdown. The dress she had worn to greet his grandfather had been inspired, making her look like a dowd, and a fat, pasty one besides, but the tantalizing contour of her elegant ankle had belied that impression. Her tiny hands were so delicate, he had been afraid he might break one just touching her when he made his bow. And the tiniest soft giggle had rushed his blood. That small noise was the reason he had made his way to the village to find a barmaid, and why he hadn't taken the wench up on her offer. She wouldn't have satisfied.

However, that was not to say he relished the likely consequence of his rash action: being married to her or dead at the wrong end of her father's pistol. No matter his skill with a gun, righteous indignation made for good aim, and there was nothing righteous about Alexander's part in this escapade. If he were caught, he might be better off just falling on his sword. His literal sword, to his literal gut.

On the other hand, a lifetime of the girl in the town coach falling onto his figurative sword might not be the worst use of a bedchamber.

Alexander blanched at the idea of this girl—what was her name?—trapped under his grandfather's noble thumb at her age. Firthley would die eventually, and she would be a rich widow, perhaps what her father intended for her security, but until then, her life would be unbearable. There was nothing his grandfather could do with such a young bride that wouldn't be traumatic for the poor girl. He had trouble comprehending the man's motivation.

Unless his plan was to disinherit Alexander, which would be fine with the reluctant earl. If he hadn't lost everything when Napoleon marched into Greece, and his mother's mother hadn't insisted before she died that he honor his patrimony, he would yet be in bed with his mistress in Crete, and the House of Lords could go hang.

Ah, Helena. There was a subject worth contemplating on this interminable road. Far better than the turn of this girl's ankle or the shape of her body beneath the form-fitting pelisse. Or replaying the sound of her voice and her laughter. Or questioning why he was driving her across country without benefit of a chaperone. Or trying to remember what the Devil her name was.

Curled into the corner of the comfortable coach, Charlotte huddled underneath the lap robe, tucking it around her shoulders, hiding her hands underneath the sable. It really was far too cold to have started a journey across country. If Lord Herrendon hadn't discovered her in the stables, she would be an icicle by now and her mare, too. It really was lucky he had come along, not that she would tell him that. Even more providential, he had brought his own carriage to Brittlestep Manor instead of riding with his grandfather.

His grandfather. Her shiver had nothing to do with the temperature; the marquess gave her the fidgets. Just the thought of him touching her nude body made her want to cast up her accounts, and no matter where they were or what they were doing, he seemed to look nowhere but her chest. At least he had taken no liberties, but that was probably because she had made certain they were never alone.

Lord Herrendon, on the other hand, was easily as handsome as a masterwork. A Grecian statue. An Italian painting. A hero in a romantic novel. She could imagine him doing all sorts of things to her nude body. The pictures she conjured were a bit indistinct, but she could certainly envision him kissing her. He would be *experienced*. And his lips wouldn't be dry or slobbery.

What her mother would do if she caught even a hint of Charlotte's thoughts! She shivered again.

It really was rather dull here in the carriage by herself. If Lord Herrendon had woken his driver, they might be happily... discussing... something. If she had known she would be traveling in the comfort of a carriage, she might have brought one of the books her mother wouldn't allow her to read.

She opened the window to the driver's box and spoke as loudly as she could, to be heard over the whistling wind.

"Are you not cold?"

"Of course I am cold."

"Perhaps you should rest the horses and come inside to warm yourself."

"Do you wish to be in Bristol before your parents catch us up?"

"Of course I do."

"Then hold your tongue and let me drive."

She closed the window, as it really was far too frigid. Only a moment or two later, she opened it again.

"Is there not an inn where we can stop for a moment for... well... er... perhaps... footwarmers? Yes, footwarmers. And I'm hungry."

"If you need to answer the call of nature, I can stop at the side of the road, but it may not be comfortable." With darkness all around, there was no way he could see the blush filling her cheeks, but it must have been present in her voice when she replied, "No... I mean... that is... I expect I can wait."

The humor in his tone was offensive in its own right. "Good. I will stop at the next such establishment I find, and we can have coals added to the footwarmers and buy a pasty or two to soothe your stomach. But we will have to be on our way as soon as we change horses, and you will have to stay in the carriage once you have... relieved your discomfort."

"But it's cold!" she persisted.

"Then it will behoove you to close the window," he snapped.

She shut it with a bang. Horrible man.

∾

"Here is your ticket," he said, handing her a card that would take her to Pembroke. When she opened her reticule to find she had not brought enough money for the fare, Lord Herrendon had purchased it on her behalf, leaving her enough ready coin to exchange it for one on the packet boat to London, if Lord Herrendon would only take his leave. When she began telling him the lie she had dreamed up during the carriage ride—a friend from school on her deathbed—he had held up his hand.

"The less I know about your plans the better. I would prefer to tell your father as few falsehoods as possible."

With a harrumph, she turned her back on him, only to feel his greatcoat drape over her shoulders.

"I'll buy another in the morning before I return to London."

"London?" Even she could hear the quaver in her voice. If he found her in London, he might tell her parents her true direction. Her adventure would be over before it began. But there was no reason to turn back yet. Perhaps he would be barred from Polite Society; his grandparents were in trade, after all.

"It would be suicidal to return to your father's house now, do you not agree?"

"I suppose." Shifting to settle the coat more comfortably on her shoulders, she turned back. "It is very kind of you to make the loan of your coat." Encountering the coins and notes stuffed into the pocket, she started to speak, but he held a finger up to her lips.

"You cannot start a journey with a thin coat or empty purse. I shall be tucked up in a warm room above a pub in short order." The sound of a ship's bell broke through the late afternoon chill, the docks frantic around them. He chucked her under the chin like she was a child, his thumb barely grazing her cheek. "I've purchased the use of a cabin, so do as I say and keep the door tightly locked." She nodded. "You'd better go, Miss..." he trailed off.

She sniffed, if only to keep from blushing and pursing her

mouth for a kiss. "If you cannot be bothered to remember my name, I hardly think you worth the reminder. Thank you for the transport, *Lord Herrendon*."

She marched to the gangplank and started onto the ship. When she turned her head to see if the way was clear to scurry back and exchange her ticket, his grin enveloped her. At his wink, she turned her nose up and marched on.

CHAPTER SEVEN

January 1, 1804
London, England

"I simply do not understand, Charlotte, why your mother cannot present you herself, nor how you came to be here, when you should be in Somerset until after Twelfth Night. You were not expected in Town until at least the tenth of January, and then, you were to arrive at your father's town house with your parents."

Her father's aunt, Lady Noakes, tapped her fingernail on the invitation card for the Queen's Drawing Room, turban and jowls quivering in contrary motion as she shook her head against the tale her great-niece had been spinning for a quarter-hour.

Charlotte was finally warm after almost a full day in Lord Herrendon's carriage, then another day on the water to Pembroke and five more to London, and a full night under three blankets in one of Aunt Henny's guest bedchambers. Upon delivery by hack, Charlotte had begged a bath and good night's rest before she confronted the problem of her great-aunt's incisive mind and sharp tongue.

Her stomach had been too unsettled to eat the night before, but hunger had finally won out over nerves. Now, seated on a silk-covered shepherdess chair in the exquisitely appointed blue parlor of the former Lord Noakes' town house, drinking tea as hot as she could make it, Charlotte only just managed to maintain her decorum instead of stuffing teacakes into her mouth whole.

"I told you, Aunt Henny, she's having one of her 'spells,' and she insisted Papa stay. They both agreed I might come ahead, in case Mother remains indisposed. It would be a shame to miss my chance at the Drawing Room and the greater portion of my own Season to indulge Mother's imperceptible illness, do you not think?"

Lady Noakes' lips pursed. "One never knows when the Queen will next hold a Drawing Room."

Charlotte motioned toward the invitation in her great-aunt's hand. "And I need a new sponsor. Mother explained it all in the letter."

"It seems rather... strange, Charlotte." Aunt Henny was no fool, but neither was Charlotte. She could have gone to any of half a dozen women in her family, but she had chosen the one with the most power among the doyennes and the most active dislike of her mother. And the one least likely to know about the plan to marry her off to a man with one foot in the grave. Charlotte had also had the presence of mind to forge a note from Lady Effingale, who had, foolishly, taught her daughter to write in the same precise copperplate hand.

"Strange or not, Aunt Henny, the Drawing Room is in a sennight, and I must replace the wardrobe that was lost when my trunk fell off the coach. I've only two dresses, and neither the required court gown."

Aunt Henny let the letter fall into her lap. "I have no idea what kind of game you are playing, Charlotte, but you are correct in one thing: one does not decline an invitation to attend royalty. There may be no other chance. I'll write to your parents this afternoon, but it will be difficult to arrange court dress so quickly. We will send for the *modiste* and see what can be done."

Charlotte hid a triumphant smile in her teacup. "Thank you, Aunt Henny."

"I am not at all certain I should be doing this, young lady, and I suspect there is some part you are withholding, but until I find out otherwise, we shall run on the assumption you are too well-bred to lie to an old woman."

"Of course, Aunt Henny." She stuffed a piece of bread into her mouth to keep from proving her aunt wrong. Now all she had to do was purloin the letter to her parents and substitute a reply she would write herself, thanking Aunt Henny kindly for taking on the role Charlotte's mother shouldn't have abdicated in the first place. If she were very, very lucky, Charlotte might have weeks to attend parties before her parents found her. She might even find herself a husband who wasn't in his dotage.

CHAPTER EIGHT

January 18, 1804
London, England

"**D**ear cousin, how delightful it is to see you alive and well." Charlotte started at the sound of Jeremy Smithson's voice, and her face paled at his bow over her hand. Bella's brothers never came to London unless they needed a win at the card tables, and she couldn't imagine how either had secured an invitation to the queen's birthday gala. His oily voice sent shivers up the back of her neck.

"Why, it was my impression your parents had been searching for you the length and breadth of England. The last I heard, your father had returned from Scotland empty-handed. I doubt anyone considered you might have travelled to London on your own."

Charlotte looked over her shoulder to make certain her aunt was outside earshot. "Hush, Jeremy Smithson. You will speak not a word of this, or I will put it out you are a card sharp."

With a slippery smile, he asked her to dance, his voice a statement, not a question. Once settled into the minuet, he spoke into her ear each time the dance brought them close. "You will say not a word except how happy you are to see me in London." He stepped away before she could respond.

"For if you do," he continued, the next time he was close enough to whisper, "I will send a letter back to Evercreech this eve with news of your direction." At her stifled response, he only smirked.

A few measures later, he added, "And I will tell my father it is time for Bella to return home where she belongs."

"You will not," she hissed at their next encounter. "For you will not wish my father to find you in Town."

"He will make an exception, methinks, for the return of his prodigal daughter."

Since she had no adequate reply, she simply refused to respond to another of his threats. Until his voice once again slithered down her spine: "You look so lovely tonight, my dear, it makes me consider removing you to Gretna Green myself." When next they met in the center of the square, his eyes didn't leave hers. "A sizable trust you were left by your grandmother." A crescendo at the end of the tune covered the squeak in her throat when he added, "Payable upon marriage, I believe." His eyes slid up and down her form. "Not a difficult task to bed you either."

She shuddered, and his malevolent smile showed he enjoyed the entire exchange far more than was decent. Not that she should expect decency from a Smithson male.

Bowing over her hand once again, he delivered her back to her aunt, who looked down her nose. Like everyone else on the Amberly side of the family, she had no liking for the Smithsons, except for Bella.

"Lady Noakes, your gown is lovely," he attempted.

Turning her head, Lady Noakes gave him the cut indirect. A flush rose in his face, flaming the broken veins in his cheeks and nose, the result of his regular consumption of too much liquor.

Charlotte's chin followed her great aunt's, but with less daring. Smithson men did not make idle threats, and Uncle Jasper had removed Bella from the Effingales' care by magistrate before.

Before Jeremy could recover his dignity by stepping back, she heard, "Miss Amberly, I believe you promised me this dance."

Could any more blood drain from her face? Could she feel any fainter? Without turning her head, she knew it was Lord Herrendon. Her cousin, thankfully, took his leave with no further comment, except avaricious eyes staring over his shoulder as he walked away.

"Lord He-Herrendon," she stuttered, "It is... unexpected... to see you here. Did you not say you do not enjoy the social scene?"

"It is, sadly, Lord Firthley now, as my grandfather left this world almost immediately on your... departure."

She gasped. "Oh, no! I am so sorry." Her hand flew to her throat, and her thoughts raced. Shocked, yes, but she was not sorry in the least. She was free!

But wait. Had she actually killed a man in her haste to be rid of him? She had been avoiding even the slightest twinges of guilt over her midnight flight on Christmas, but if it had resulted in the marquess's untimely demise, it was not such a far jump to murder. She would hate to think she had become a murderess.

"Please, let us not dissemble," he said. "We are both better off for the loss, and it was surely not your fault he overindulged in rich food and spirits his entire life. If a man cannot survive one sharp shock to his sensibilities, he surely does not deserve to live."

"But you..." She looked around the room. "You cannot dance with your grandfather buried not even a fortnight ago. You should not be here."

"You are entirely correct about the dancing, but as to my attendance, the previous Lord Firthley went to great lengths to arrange for my invitation to venues where my parentage would not preclude attendance, so I am merely carrying out his wishes.

And with respect to my attentions to you, Miss Amberly, I only hoped to discourage the gentleman of whom you are so frightened."

"Frightened—?" She straightened her shoulders. "I am not frightened."

"Terrified, in truth. Will you take a turn about the room with me?" He stuck out his elbow. "Perhaps we might step out onto the terrace for some air? I was afraid you might faint while I watched you dancing."

"Charlotte," her aunt intoned in her most imperious voice, quite highhanded indeed, "Who is this gentleman, and why has he not asked an introduction?" Lady Noakes eyed the black armband and cravat. "Is it quite appropriate for you to be in company, Mr....?"

He bowed over Lady Noakes' hand. "Lord Firthley, and I am wholly inappropriate, I'm afraid," he said as he bowed over her hand, trying a wink, which fell short. Her mien relaxed not a jot until he said, "I simply wished to pay my respects to Miss Amberly. I am an associate of her father's, you see. We met at Brittlestep Manor some weeks ago."

"Firthley. You are the grandson from Greece, then. I was sorry to hear of your grandfather's passing. The last Lord Firthley was a fine man." At his hesitation, Lady Noakes said, "You have taken your opinion of him from your father, I see. You should know Lord Firthley regretted your father's leave-taking the rest of his life."

"I thought—" Lord Firthley began.

Lady Noakes cut him off. "I imagine you did. You may not dance with my niece and bring the scandal of your filial contempt down on her, but you may walk about the room with her, within my sight."

He inclined his head in thanks, then offered Charlotte his arm.

"I am very sorry to hear of your bereavement." She tried to

determine how best to gather details without being rude. "So, he was... er... that is to say..."

"On your dining table, face-down in the kippers, the very morning you escaped. We must have been halfway to Bristol when it happened."

Her gloved hand covered her mouth, then cradled her cheek, as though she could hold back the heat rising. "Heavens! That must have been... My mother must have..."

"I am told your mother nearly expired on the spot. Even so, she managed to arrange for the coroner to remove his body from the environs of your house, and to keep anyone from discovering you had killed your own fiancé on your way to elope with a sailor."

Charlotte looked away, sure her face could be no more red, fingers picking at her skirt. "Bella made the arrangements, I'm sure. Mother will have spent three days in a dead faint. Maybe five." Charlotte realized she had spoken aloud only when he snickered at her. She looked up. "But how do you..."

"Your father's solicitor was gentleman enough to offer me the truth, but I assure you, he insisted on my perfect discretion before he would say a word. You'll have no trouble snaring a husband out of fear you will kill him."

"But—" She dropped his arm. "What a perfectly awful thing to say! Of course I did not kill him!" After a moment's pause she asked, "Is my father... does he... I mean, was your solicitor made aware—"

"I was not, apparently, gentleman enough to be honest with your father's man about your flight from Somerset, and Lord Effingale has yet to turn up in London to call me out for it. Scotland, yes. Bristol, Portsmouth, and Pembroke, but not London. He must not wish to think his perfect angel capable of declaring herself a debutante, replacing her own mother, and forcing her presence on the queen unbidden."

"That's not—"

His brow arched over his right eye, and the corner of his lips followed. "No?"

Charlotte cleared her throat and stared past his shoulder. "I had an invitation."

"Truly, I am amazed word of your come-out has not made it to Somerset in the weeks since your departure. Did your aunt not write your parents immediately upon your arrival?"

Her blush stemmed from anger, surely, not embarrassment or remorse. She would never have been forced to this deception were it not for her mother's ridiculous insistence on marrying her off to a man four times her age. Sharpening her sense of self-right-eousness, she demanded, "How is it, Sir, you find yourself at a party during your bereavement?"

"Do you wish to leave to assuage your grief, my dear, having lost your betrothed?" At her narrow-eyed stare, he just chuckled. "Just so. As I said, my grandfather made quite an effort to arrange invitations to any event where a foreigner might not cause a scandal."

"You are hardly a foreigner, Lord Herrendon—Firthley. You are a Marloughe and a marquess."

"Yes," he whispered into her ear, "but my mother was an opera singer."

She stumbled on both her words and her hem. "An oper—I mean... goodness!"

"*Singer*, my girl, not dancer," he said, steadying her. "In other parts of Europe, quite celebrated, in fact. My father was hardly the first to attempt an alliance, but was the only gentleman to be granted one. I understand my grandfather was sent quite mad by their elopement, cutting my father off without a penny, swearing to never allow him to inherit. Sadly for the last Lord Firthley, he was not able to produce the requisite spare, so upon my father's death, he was saddled with me."

"I'm sure he would not say—would not have said—*saddled*, my lord." Charlotte was not at all certain of that. "I am sure he was quite pleased to know his heir was so..." She reached for the right words. "...cultured and... artistic."

Lord Firthley threw his head back and laughed aloud, and Charlotte looked around and over her shoulder. His outburst did not go unmarked, nor had his attendance in the earliest days of mourning. She would never find a husband at this rate.

"Artistic, indeed. You have a charming way with words, my dear." He left the conversation there, walking in silence. Looking across the room at her aunt, he whispered, "Your dragon is not looking. Shall we risk a sojourn on the terrace?"

"Perhaps we—" There was no finishing the thought before he swept her past the diamond-paned French doors, onto the quiet terrace, remarkably free of other couples. The night was positively balmy for late January, and the sky clear enough to count the stars. Torches set along the edges of the walkway into the garden invited a promenade, but Charlotte was not so brave as to follow him into the relative darkness. She hesitated at the edge of the graveled path.

The corner of his lips turned up. "You would travel across England on horseback through a snowstorm, yet balk at taking a few steps from a ballroom?"

"Hush. You said you would not mention that where anyone might hear."

"Then I believe, Miss Amberly," he said, with a devious smile, "we must move out of earshot, for I find I must discover the secret of how such a proper young woman, raised to trust in her father's goodwill, has both the spirit and temerity to race across country to escape her fate, and can charm an otherwise intelligent man to help her."

"You are a perfect beast! A gentleman would never coerce a young lady by threat of telling her secrets."

His voice against her ear warmed her in a way no fire ever could. "Would it really be coercion, then? There is no part of you that would like to follow me into the hedge maze and ascertain what adventures I might offer?"

Shivering—surely due to the chill in the air—she said not another word as he guided her toward a bench just off the path. They could be seen if anyone looked closely, but were yet cloaked in shadow.

"It is cold," she finally said, sitting, then standing, then sitting again when he did. "We should return to the ballroom."

He shrugged out of his jacket and offered to place it around her shoulders. In horror, she scooted as far away from him as she could without falling off the end of the bench. "I cannot wear your clothing, Sir! What would people think?"

"They would think you were chilled, and I was polite enough to accommodate."

"*Accommodate*. That is exactly what they would think." Searching the darkness for anyone who might be looking or listening, she demanded, "We must return to the ballroom!"

Standing, he restored his tailcoat to his shoulders, then offered his hand. Without taking it, she turned away.

"No? Do you not wish to be shut of me? I confess, Miss Amberly, I am not sure how to make you happy, and where women are concerned, that state of affairs is unfamiliar."

Her mouth opened and closed on words that would not form until she finally clenched her jaw and took his hand. As he led her back to the party, he murmured in her ear, "You may be certain, Miss Amberly, this will not be the last adventure I will offer. Might I call on you at your aunt's residence on the morrow?"

Without saying a word, she glared at him, nodding her head.

CHAPTER NINE

The next day...

"So, how did you come to be in London rather than Pembroke? Was Pembroke not the destination you gave while we were traveling to Bristol?"

"It is entirely too chilly to be out driving. Are you not solid ice?" Her hand dug a bit farther into her fur muff, flushing at Lord Firthley's shrewd question, more so when he winked at her.

"I might have icicles hanging from my eyebrows before we return," Lord Firthley said, "which I prefer to taking tea under the eagle eye of your chaperone. Will you answer my question?"

Charlotte pulled her muffler higher on her cheeks to hide her discomfiture. Fortunately, the sun was only a weak source of warmth, bright enough to suggest a ride in Hyde Park, but not to cut through a sharp wind. Her aunt had suggested they stay inside in the drawing room, but he was not particularly amenable, and Aunt Henny was unwilling to discourage the interest of a marquess.

She turned away from him on the high seat of his phaeton,

taking one hand out of her muff to hold on when she scooted away from him and his invasive questions.

"You must be aware that asking a lady to divulge information she would prefer to keep private is quite rude. Or do they not teach gentlemen such things in Greece?"

His laughter boomed across the frozen, gray landscape, no other carriages or people to delay the sound. "Another thing they teach gentlemen in Greece is that when a lady only claims the designation when it is convenient, and otherwise acts any way she pleases, the courtesies might be relaxed a bit." He clucked his tongue at the horses and curved around the path to turn the carriage toward her aunt's house. "And if a man can find a way past propriety with this particular model of lady, he has a chance at a very entertaining companion."

"Companion?" She raised a brow.

"What else would you have me call you? Now then, I am fairly certain your aunt had no knowledge of your plans, or I would not have had to answer for my whereabouts the night you disappeared. Will you argue semantics with me until we arrive back at your house? Shall I be forced to connive my way into a dinner invitation and ask you in front of Lady Noakes?"

"You wouldn't!"

"I would."

She wished her sniff was at his ridiculous demands and not because her nose was dripping. Turning up her frozen nostrils, she finally answered, "I was to be denied my Season to marry your grandfather. I wished to make my curtsey to the queen and attend a few parties before I was forced to wed an ol..." She snapped her mouth closed before she insulted him, then thought the better of trying to be kind. "Before I had to marry a bald, wrinkly old man who would take my dowry and touch me with those hideous claws he called hands. Just the thought was... well... I'm certain you can imagine."

"I hope never to imagine such a thing, but I find it fascinating that you have."

Her indignant squeak was lost on him, so she marshalled her outrage for a righteous tongue-lashing. "That is the rudest thing I have ever heard! I'll not say another word to you, for you are no gentleman. Take me home at once!"

"Never fear, Miss Amberly, we are no more than ten minutes away. For what it's worth, I do understand your reasons for leaving. I find it quite bold, and unaccountably intriguing. I am rather of a mind to..." He looked her up and down out of the corner of his eye. "Well, what I have in mind does not signify."

"Not. Another. Word." Charlotte burrowed more deeply into her muffler and drew her collar tighter around her ears. "You are quite the worst man I have ever met."

CHAPTER TEN

January 26, 1804
London, England

"Your actions are reprehensible! I cannot believe the nerve!"

Charlotte sat, head bowed, chafing under her father's screaming—and under her own remorse for causing him such trouble. If only he had listened when she told him she didn't want to marry Lord Firthley, especially not to solve a political problem; it was hardly her responsibility to advance the business of the nation. He had never been so unfeeling before. But he also never screamed at her, which meant she was lucky it was he, not her mother. Her mother might actually kill her.

"How did you—?"

"Are you certain you wish to ask me how I knew you have been presenting yourself at parties throughout London as if you have my permission to do so?"

"Who—?"

"It makes no matter who! I have been up and down England

looking for you. Weeks! Weeks I have been searching you out. Your mother is beside herself, can barely rise from bed, she has been so worried!"

That her mother had taken to bed was no surprise. She hardly had to be told a ribbon couldn't be matched to a reticule to find herself incapacitated. But Papa really did have more important things to do, and, until the debacle with the late Lord Firthley, had always been the one to take up on her side in every family argument. If she had threatened to run away, rather than simply doing it, he might have even understood the depth of her aversion.

She buckled under her own remorse for causing him such trouble. If only he had listened when she told him she didn't want to marry Lord Firthley, especially not to solve a political problem; it was hardly her responsibility to advance the business of the nation. He had never been so unfeeling before.

But wait. Taken to her bed? "So... Mother is not with you?"

"I've sent a letter, so you may expect her within the week, and do not doubt I will hand you over to her with no compunction, you devious, deceitful girl. And this letter will not be pilfered by a thieving hoyden!"

Charlotte drew in a sharp breath. An entire week for Lady Effingale to marshal her anger? Charlotte was no longer sure she would be standing after her mother's punishment was imposed for leaving her betrothed behind, running away with the man's heir, arranging her own presentation, and attending countless parties with one of Mother's least favorite people as chaperone. If she were fortunate, the death would be quick.

"Thankfully, I have found a means of containing the potential scandal before she arrives and proceeds to murder. Though I cannot say I am pleased with the solution."

"Will you send me back to Evercreech, then?"

"And have you disappear from a posting inn like an outlaw?

No. I've had an offer for your hand, which you will accept with alacrity, and you will be married within a fortnight."

Her head popped up. "But... no! What? You can't—"

"I can. Once you have wed, you will return to Evercreech with your husband."

Her mouth fell open. "Ever...? No... oh, no... you cannot mean to marry me to *Jeremy*!"

She would be better off marrying ten Lord Firthleys than Jeremy Smithson. She couldn't count the blood, bruises, and breaks he had left on his sister, not to mention the manner in which he made his questionable living. Her dowry would be lost in a card game in a matter of days, leaving her to starve under his heavy hand forevermore.

"As he is the only offer you have, and certainly the fastest possible answer to the question of your inexcusable behavior, oh, yes, I do."

"You would give me to *him*, after everything he has done to Bella?"

He gritted his teeth and pointed a finger at her. "You have put yourself in this position, Charlotte Amberly, not I. Do not *dare* blame me for the fact you are now unmarriageable. I will ensure you live close enough for me to watch over him, and I will make his income dependent on your happiness, but you will *not* blame this fiasco on me. You will not!"

The tears welling up might have been anger or fear or frustration or despair, but regardless, there was no stopping them. "He is my cousin!"

"And a ne'er-do-well. At this point, Charlotte, that cannot be helped. As soon as anyone finds out what you have been up to— and I assure you, he will make it known within minutes of me rejecting his suit—you will be ruined. Utterly ruined. You will never be able to set foot in Town again."

"But—" She couldn't choke out any more objections through the sobbing about to start.

"I will listen to not another word of insolence. You will marry when I say, where I say, and to whom I say, or you will be confined to Bedlam!"

With that, he grasped her elbow, paying no attention to the tears streaking her face. When she tried to pull herself away, his grip strengthened until she thought her arm would break. Stumbling after him to her room, then shoved without ceremony through the door, she was horrified to hear the lock turn.

Banging on the door, yelling to be let out, made no difference. Kicking it only bruised her toe. She leaned her forehead against the door and tried to slow the tears. Weeping would not help anything. She gathered deep, sobbing breaths until the choking abated.

"He will not change his mind, Charlotte."

She yelped in surprise, having assumed the room was empty, jumping as she turned. Sitting quietly in a corner, embroidering, was her cousin Bella.

"What are you doing here?" Charlotte asked.

"Uncle Howard was concerned that Aunt Minerva would..."

"Send you back to Uncle Jasper."

"Yes."

Charlotte plopped down onto the chair next to Bella's seat on the loveseat and turned up the lamp.

"Though with all the trouble Jeremy is causing..." Bella sighed. "I'm sure my father is too busy counting your dowry to bother with me."

"How can they—"

Bella just stared. "Have you ever known my father to leave a penny lay when he might put it in his pocket?"

"Well, no, but I am his niece. How can he wish to..." Charlotte trailed off, reminded of all the horrific things that had been done to Uncle Jasper's own daughter. Far worse than marrying her to a good-for-nothing, though now that she was old enough, that day would come.

At the look on her cousin's face, Bella said, simply, "Quite."

"I cannot marry Jeremy!" Charlotte stood and began pacing. "How can I...?" She went to the window and pushed it open, looking to see how she could escape.

"He has a footman posted."

Snorting out her frustration through her nose, Charlotte slammed the window closed and began pacing again.

"He will let you out," Charlotte wheedled. "You can steal the—"

"I will not! You have made your own mess, Charlotte."

"But you always—"

"I will do whatever I can to argue your father out of this course, but I will not move against him in such an underhanded way. He has kept me as safe as he can my entire life, a debt of which I was reminded when Aunt Minerva wanted to throw me out in the snow less than a month ago. He has treated me as a second daughter, and while you may discount that gift, I will not."

"So that is why you are here?"

"Indeed. And with Jeremy in London, John and my father can't be far behind. I will happily stay locked in my room until they are gone."

"But for witnessing my marriage to the brother who so enjoys beating you bloody every time he can, you mean."

Bella winced and shrank back into the chair. "I do hope it won't come to that."

Charlotte was having trouble maintaining sympathy with anyone unwilling to change this course.

"Surely, Aunt Minerva won't allow it," Bella said, "She hates my father and Jeremy. She will talk sense into your father."

"She will accept the first marriage contract offered, if it will keep her from scandal, and I've already made enough scandal for a lifetime." Charlotte snarled in a manner more fit for a mean-spirited gentleman than a well-bred young lady.

There was no arguing the point.

CHAPTER ELEVEN

The next day...

"I do apologize, my lord, Miss Amberly is not receiving visitors today."

Alexander stared blankly at the butler. He had seen Charlotte every day for a week, and they had made plans for a trip to the British Museum this afternoon.

"Perhaps you do not understand. I've made an appointment to see her."

"She is not receiving visitors today, my lord."

"Is she ill?"

"She is not receiving visitors."

"Has she left a message for me? For Lord Firthley?" He repeated his name for the second time in as many minutes.

"No, my lord. Had she left a message, I would have provided it."

"I don't understand."

"It is quite simple, my lord. Miss Amberly is not receiving today. Perhaps if you were to return another day."

"I'm afraid I must insist you tell me if she is unwell."

"I'm afraid I cannot do so, my lord. I can only say that she—"

"Is not receiving today."

"Yes, my lord."

The butler wouldn't shut the door in his face, but would stand in the same position all day to keep him out.

"Might I speak to her aunt? Lady Noakes?"

"Lady Noakes is not receiving, my lord."

Alexander ground his teeth. "Is anyone receiving?"

"If you would like to wait, I will see if Lord Effingale is available."

Charlotte's father? In Town? No wonder Charlotte wasn't receiving. He had probably horsewhipped her.

"No. No, I will come back another day. Thank you for..."

On the other hand, it might not be a bad idea to present his apologies and his version of things to Lord Effingale sooner rather than later. Effingale's solicitor, when he appeared with the sad news of the late Lord Firthley's demise, had been amenable enough to Alexander's lie about leaving Evercreech in the middle of the night to respond to a crisis on his estate. It would be smart to reinforce the story, and wise to thank Effingale for the discreet handling of his grandfather's death.

"On second thought, I would like to speak to Lord Effingale, if you would be so kind." He removed his hat and gloves as he entered, handing them over with his cane as he was shown into the receiving room off the foyer. After the butler left, he strolled about the room, too keyed up to sit, but not anxious enough to pace.

The matching green and amber T'ang vases on either side of the hearth held stems of orange bird-of-paradise, the colors and patterns played out in the carpet and drapes. The curios on the shelves were lovely, but none with the value of the vases, only prettily made ceramics and porcelains, a bronze figurine here, a filigree statuette there. A stone bust of some unknown ancestor had either been carved at three-quarter size or the original subject had a suspiciously small head.

Swiveling at the sound of the door sliding open, he nearly knocked the bust off its pedestal, managing to keep it upright by shoving the palm of his hand into the poor man's nose. Thus, Lord Effingale found him, seemingly caressing a man's cheek.

"Lord Firthley," his host said, his tone flat, gaze traveling between Alexander's face and fingers. Alexander rapidly set the statue aright and placed his hand behind his back, as though his intent all along had been merely to bow.

"Lord Effingale, I thank you for agreeing to see me when I've sent no notice."

"Indeed." Lord Effingale gestured to a seat and took a chair directly across a tea table. "It is not altogether convenient, but I can spare a few moments. I would have called on you in the next few days, in any case, to express my condolences."

"Very kind." Alexander had every intention of bolstering whatever story Charlotte might have told, and making sure he stayed on good terms with Lord Effingale, though he couldn't explain why it was important. Just now, however, he found himself struggling for words.

Thankfully, Lord Effingale seemed more inclined to coherent discussion. "My aunt tells me you've shown a great partiality to my daughter since she has been in Town."

"Partiali—well... Miss Amberly is certainly... I am not entirely sure I would say..."

"Yet," the man said, sitting back, crossing his ankle over his knee, "my solicitor assures me you had no knowledge of her direction or her plans to escape Brittlestep Manor. 'You have naught but the barest memory of the chit.'"

Alexander swallowed hard. He had only rarely chosen women with living fathers, and this was why. "Yes... well... er..."

"How did she do it, Lord Firthley?"

"Ahem... do what, Sir?"

"Convince a man who seemed to possess a modicum of intellect to take her to Bristol or Portsmouth or wherever it was you delivered her before you stopped at your estate on the way to London?"

"I'm sure I've not... That is to say..." *Good God, what was I thinking, requesting this meeting? Where in the name of Heaven was that modicum of intellect?*

"I know my daughter, Lord Firthley. Whatever she told you was most certainly a lie, and while most often well-intentioned, she is the most persuasive young lady in Christendom. She spends every penny of her pin money as soon as it is in her pocket, so she couldn't have paid you, nor do you need her quarterly allowance. I cannot believe she would have offered up her virtue, nor that you would have taken it, but there is no denying you complied with her plan, whatever it was; that I can see by the look on your face. So what was it?"

"She didn't... I mean... I say, this is not at all why I hoped to speak with you." If he had known the direction this interview would take, he wouldn't have even knocked on the door.

"I will give you some credit, Lord Firthley. Charlotte was not buried beneath a snowdrift by morning, which I'm sure she would have been, had you not forced her stubborn carcass into a carriage. And you didn't take a driver, so presumably, you kept your hands on the ribbons and not her person."

"I... of course, I..." Alexander's lips just kept flapping, though he could push no more words through them.

"And to be fair, there is blame to be lain at many feet, mine own included. Was it merely concern for her safety that set you off in your carriage in the small hours?"

"Well, there is no question... that is... estate business. It was estate business." If he said it often enough, perhaps someone in the room would believe him.

"It most certainly was not. She is ruined, nonetheless, you understand."

There was that. If anyone discovered what she had done, the poor girl would be consigned to a solitary life in the country the rest of her life. If anyone discovered his part, he would, rightly, find himself a social pariah—though to be fair, not nearly as long as she would. Assuming, of course, the man in front of him didn't call him out and run him through, which was entirely his privilege. There was no help for it. Alexander had no right to lie to Lord Effingale, nor pretend the situation was anything but dire.

"I have not spoken of the matter, nor will I. And I can assure you, she was quite untouched when I left her. You have no reason to fear I will participate in any plan to do harm to her reputation... nor any other part of her."

"What you will or will not do is irrelevant, Lord Firthley, for the matter is not unknown to all. That, Sir, is why my daughter is not receiving today, nor will she be entertaining any gentlemen in the future." Lord Effingale stood, stepping over to the decanters. "She will be married by the end of the week."

"What?" Alexander shot up out of his chair, pacing without thinking to the fireplace and back. "Married? To whom?"

Lord Effingale poured two glasses of brandy and handed one to Alexander, who took it without thinking and set it down on the table.

"Not that it is your concern, Lord Firthley, but she will be wed to her cousin, Mr. Smithson."

"Her cousin? That scoundrel?"

"Yes, that is the one."

"But she is afraid of him!"

"With good reason."

Lord Effingale waved him back to a seat, and Alexander felt

his legs fold underneath him, again, purely by instinct. Or inexplicable fear.

He handed the glass back to Alexander. "My daughter ran off in the night, made her way to London alone, lied to my aunt—and by extension, the Queen of England—to have herself presented without the knowledge of her parents, and has been traipsing about Town like an untrained puppy. Someone has to marry her, and her cousin is the closest available male who will make no objection. And, by the by, he has discovered her various deceptions, and, like any good scoundrel, will use the information to his benefit." He took a long draught of his drink. "And, in this case, there is money to be had."

"You mean to say he would..."

"Aye. If there is advantage, he will, and, in this case, there is money to be had. I have only one other option, you see, Lord Firthley."

"What other option is that, Sir?"

"I have an unsigned marriage contract with the Marquess of Firthley, and a man so named who played a key role in her ruination."

Alexander could spit no more than a syllable at a time from his mouth. "But... I... she..."

Lord Effingale raised one brow. "Yes?"

"You cannot expect... how you can just hand her over to that havey-cavey... The rumors..."

"Every one true and more, I assure you. My wife's brother is the worst man I have ever encountered, and his sons have not fallen far from the tree. I do not relish the decision I am forced to, Lord Firthley, but as they say, my daughter has made her bed and now she must lie in it."

The thought of that beautiful girl in this particular bed was more than Alexander could stand. "I find that remarkably callous, to just hand over your daughter to a man like that."

"I have but one other option, Lord Firthley, and you seem disinclined to do anything but sputter. Now, as to this other business you wished to discuss? Was it of some urgency, or might we make an appointment for later in the week?"

"It is... I mean... I suppose we can..."

"Good." Lord Effingale took to his feet and smoothed down his trousers. "It will prove to be quite a busy week, with my wife arriving in a few days and a wedding to arrange. I will have my secretary be in contact to arrange a time, if I may."

"Of course."

As Lord Effingale walked to the door to show his guest out, Alexander quaffed the last of the brandy, thumped his glass onto the table, and said, "I'll do it. I'll marry her."

CHAPTER TWELVE

January 29, 1804
London, England

"Mother!" Charlotte's brows drew together as she threw yet another argument at Lady Effingale's reflection in the looking glass. "Why must I marry at all? No one knows anything, and there are months of parties left in the Season."

Lady Effingale stopped combing her daughter's hair, looking as though she would speak, but Bella's soft voice started first. From the chair near the dressing screen, where she was brushing Charlotte's slippers, she said, "Because my brother will ruin you if you do not."

"Quite right, Isabella, dear. Is that a tear in the sole of that shoe?" Lady Effingale snatched the left slipper from Bella's hand, and the two girls performed twin eye rolls in the mirror. "You will marry in two days' time, as your father has arranged, and we will say nothing more about it."

"But I don't want to!"

"And I care not at all what you want, Charlotte Amberly. You have had 'what you want' for nearly a month, and the only thing to come of it is an offer to destroy the reputation of this entire family. You have made a mockery of everything I ever taught you, and ruined yourself into the bargain. Let this be your punishment."

"To be married to a man I hate for the rest of my life?"

"Yes."

"But—"

"Not another word, Charlotte. You might have stopped this before it started by exercising the slightest bit of restraint. Isabella, please check that the lace has been properly tacked onto the green gown. There wasn't time to see to it before I left."

Bella took the dress in question to the corner, where she settled herself on a shepherdess chair almost the same green as the bodice. Once the lace was reattached, she tightened a seam.

"Must I really attend a party and pretend to be happy about marrying in haste and repenting in leisure?"

Lady Effingale let out an exasperated huff and wrenched the brush through Charlotte's hair, inspiring a yelp. When Charlotte reached up to discover whether she now had a bald spot, her mother slapped her hand away.

"You will attend the party. You will stand up for every dance with your new betrothed and make enough lovesick calves' eyes to put a herd of beeves to shame. And you will marry in two days' time, whether you like it or not!" The boar-bristle brush caught on a tangle and brushed through it with no concern for Charlotte's wincing.

"But—"

Lady Effingale grasped Charlotte's hair and pulled her head back to glare upside-down. "You will do exactly what I say, Charlotte, or I will turn you out with nothing. Do you understand me? No dowry, no money, not even a pelisse to keep you warm. You wish to run away from your family? Very well. I will let you go, but you will not use Amberly or Effingale money to do it. We will see how long you last on the streets of London."

Shoving Charlotte's head forward, she used the brush to turn a curl around her hand, tipping her head to gauge whether it was too wide to frame her daughter's face. Apparently, she decided it was, as she separated it into strands, using a pin to secure one ringlet to the crown of Charlotte's head. Charlotte's mutinous expression in the looking glass finally resolved itself to resignation and despair.

"Perhaps it will not be so bad, Charlotte," Bella offered. "You will be living close by. You can visit any time you like."

"Easy enough for you to say!" Charlotte shouted as she turned, locks of hair flying about her face like driving rain. "You'll be living in my room, in my house, with no unspeakable husband to tell you what to do!" At that, her screeching turned to sobs, and she put her head down on the dressing table and cried.

Bella sat quietly with her needlework, waiting for the storm to pass. Charlotte's fits of temper, while fiery, had no lasting heat.

Lady Effingale, on the other hand, would have none of it.

"That is the outside of enough, girl. I will have no truck with this unseemly behavior. Stop that sniveling, sit up straight, and act like the lady you were raised to be."

Finally, after several long minutes of her mother's toe tapping in an angry rhythm, Charlotte sat up and glared at Bella in the mirror.

Two hours later, Charlotte was handed down first from the carriage, holding her emerald green silk skirt and black velvet cloak just slightly higher than her slipper, to avoid the muddy street. Throwing her shoulders back, head high, she marched to the front door of the Popham's town house, not stopping until her father snapped sharply, "Charlotte, you will wait for the rest of us."

Once Lady Effingale, and finally Bella, were on the walk, straightening their clothes from the carriage ride, Lord and Lady Effingale joined arms and led the two girls to the door. Immediately upon entering, before she had even removed her cloak, a familiar voice spoke in her ear as a set of large hands helped her off with her outerwear. She shuddered at the contact.

"You look charming, my dear, and so lovely in green. I believe this shade perfectly matches your eyes."

Tossing his hands off her shoulders, spinning on her heel, she narrowed the eyes that matched her outfit and her jewels and snarled, as quietly as she could manage, "You do not have permission to touch me, Sir, and I do not appreciate your forward behavior."

"But, dearest..." Lord Firthley smiled in that infernally appealing way, one side of his lips turned up, and his eyes sparkling the way they did when he laughed. "Surely you cannot object to your betrothed merely touching your arm."

She turned away from his low bow with a harrumph. When he offered his elbow to lead her to the ballroom, she stared at it like he was hiding a snake in his sleeve, until her mother grasped her hand and placed it under Lord Firthley's arm, hissing in her ear, "You. Will. Not. Make. A. Scene. Smile, Charlotte Amberly, or I will make you wish you had."

With a beleaguered sigh, she allowed herself to be led away by the horrible man who had offered for her without once mentioning his intentions.

When they entered the ballroom, the buzz of conversation stopped, then restarted, all eyes trained on her. Jeremy had clearly begun his campaign to see her ruined, but Lord Firthley merely patted her hand, smiled down at her with genuine pleasure, and said, "If nothing else, we will be amused all evening by the assembled lords and ladies who cannot decide whether to vilify you or fawn over me."

Charlotte hardened her face into the sharp smile she had perfected years ago, and said, "Perhaps the rest of the assemblage will toady to you, my lord, but if I am to be your wife, you should not come to expect it from me."

With a chuckle, he brushed his gloved hand across her cheek and whispered in her ear, "I will expect many things from you as my wife, my sweet; toadying is not one of them."

At her gasp, watching the blush fill her cheeks, he nodded in satisfaction and led her to the dance floor

CHAPTER THIRTEEN

B ella took up her usual position in a quiet corner. She had been acting as Charlotte's companion so long she was quite familiar with being ignored, though being ignored in London was new. She should not even be here, as she would not have a come-out until next year, if at all. It was rather a ridiculous exercise, in Bella's opinion, because she wasn't pretty enough to attract the attention of potential husbands, and her dowry was laughable. Not to mention she had no idea what to say to strangers of either gender. She would rather clean chamber pots for pirates than speak to people she didn't know.

Still, it was not so much a trial to sit and listen to the music, watch the pretty gowns and jewels, steal glances at the handsome gentlemen who would never ask her to dance. Her feet mimicked the steps of the cotillion, so ensconced in Mozart, she didn't notice the man coming up to bow before her. When she did, she shot up out of her seat, searching the crowd for her uncle.

"Dear Sister," Jeremy sneered, grabbing her elbow before she could run. "I believe we must dance, lest the company believe there to be bad blood between us. There are already unavoidable questions about why the Smithson chit does not reside at home, nor enjoy the escort of her loving brothers who would, of course, stop at nothing to protect her from harm."

Blood drained from her face, and she dredged up a fake smile. Bella felt so sick she thought she might cast up her accounts in the ballroom. She tried to back away, saying, "You must let me go, Jeremy. I've had the headache all day and am afraid I will be sick."

His cold eyes bore into hers, setting her cowering before she could remind herself not to react. "You will do nothing of the sort, for if you cause a commotion, I will remove you from the party and take you directly home to Father. Which is where you will go soon, in any case, most likely to prepare for your own wedding." She shrank to the size of a walnut. With no further argument, she followed him onto the floor.

As always, Jeremy was masterful at appearing to enjoy the entertainments, while making her life unbearable under his breath, anytime they came close enough in the dance to hiss vile words into her ear.

"I do not appreciate being made to look a fool, and you may say so to our lovely cousin."

As she started, "But I have nothing..." the dance parted them.

At the next turn, he said, "I will not sleep until she is finished in England."

No argument would satisfy him, but if he believed Bella compliant, he might leave her alone a while, without convincing their father she required 'correction.'

"I will decry her until her precious marquess cannot stand the sight of her."

As Bella stepped away in the figure of the dance, her brother was jerked out of the formation with a yelp, his face shocked and arms pinwheeling backward. While Lord Firthley marched Jeremy toward the doors to the terrace, Charlotte grasped Bella's arm from behind, whisked her away to the ladies' withdrawing room, and locked the door behind them. Before they had taken two steps off the dance floor, the entire room had fallen silent, including the string quartet.

"Charlotte, you cannot allow him to make such a scene! Aunt Minerva will—"

"There is no taking back the scene now, and my mother will button her lip if the marquess tells her to do so, and he assures me he will. Jeremy was making threats against me, I suppose, and to take you home to your father if you didn't comply with some dastardly plan?"

Bella nodded, tears welling up in her eyes now that the fear had partially abated.

"I thought you might expire on the spot, so white was your face. There is no need to be afraid of him now, for Ale—Lord Firthley is quite livid about the entire thing, and holds Jeremy responsible. He pledged to me not three minutes ago he would stop Jeremy's interference." Her voice grew gravelly and vicious as she added, "With a pistol, most likely."

"What have you told him? You cannot tell Lord Firthley about —Aunt Minerva will murder me!"

"Hush," Charlotte said, pulling Bella into her arms and stroking her back while Bella finally dissolved into quiet weeping. "My mother will do nothing I do not tell her, for I will be a marchioness in two days, and no longer subject to her meddling."

Once Bella's sobs abated, Charlotte dried her cousin's eyes and adjusted her stick-straight hair, as always, falling from its pins in the warm ballroom.

"Now, before my mother has apoplexy in company, we must go out there and pretend there is nothing for the *ton* to gossip about, until we can make our escape."

"But there most certainly—"

"Is not. Now then."

Charlotte looped her arm in Bella's and once again utilized her counterfeit smile, directing Bella through the halls until they made it to the refreshment room, with a much smaller crowd. Even so, the room stilled when they walked through the door.

Uncle Howard stepped up to meet them, bowing to his daughter and niece with his own false face, offering, "You look peaked, my dear. A cup of punch, perhaps?" He walked both girls thorough the hushed crowd and had a footman pour punch, handing the glass to Bella, squeezing her fingers in a small show of support as he did.

Conversation began to fill the room again, assuredly now all about them. Uncle Howard whispered, "I am having the carriage brought round. Your mother is waiting in the foyer with your wraps, and Lord Firthley will meet us once he has... made... arrangements."

"Arrangements? Surely you cannot mean—"

Bella's hand shook until she thought the punch would spill on her gown, so she held her arm out just slightly to keep it from being upset. Just as her uncle nodded to confirm her worst fear, something bumped her from behind and sent both cup and punch flying from her trembling fingers, drenching everyone nearby, most notably the hostess and the gentleman to whom she had been conversing—the Duke of Lanceley. When that illustrious gentleman turned his gaze on her, yellow liquid dripping from his nose onto his starched cravat, Bella squeaked and ran.

CHAPTER FOURTEEN

February 2, 1804
London, England

"It is miraculous he still wants to marry you at all, Charlotte, after what this family has put him through the past few days."

"That's perfectly fine! I don't want to marry him anyway!"

"You would rather marry my brother?" Bella asked quietly from her usual corner.

"I would rather not marry anyone! I shall be an old spinster with too many cats, and live in a cottage in the wilds of Yorkshire until I die!" She held her head high and threw her arms out dramatically. "I shall live my own life and make my own decisions!"

"And you will do so with no money, Charlotte," her mother snapped, "for you cannot collect on your trust for a dozen more years unless you marry, and if you jilt that young man after he fought a duel to save you from ruin, I will throw you from this house myself."

"And me," Bella murmured. "He saved me, too."

Charlotte huffed and sat back down at her dressing table. "That is precisely why I shouldn't marry him. He will have no good name left, nor will I. I can retire to the country to avoid the disgrace. He can say he escaped the parson's mousetrap and a sure life of infamy, and the scandal will die down. If we marry, we will be the Filthy Firthleys forevermore."

"Do not be ridiculous," Lady Effingale said, gathering up Charlotte's hair to braid it. "As long as you marry a marquess, your reputation will suffer not a jot." To distract both girls, she said, "If you are a good girl and are quiet, I will tell you what you have been asking me since you were thirteen, hoyden that you are."

Charlotte's eyes widened, then lit from within. "Really?"

"You will be a bride tomorrow, so you must know what will happen in your bedchamber with your husband." Bella's face turned red, and she stared at her hands, but in the mirror, Charlotte marked her surreptitious interest. Both girls were silent, even for breathing.

Sliding the brush gently through Charlotte's hair, her mother began, "You mustn't believe the silliness of servants when they tell tales. It cannot be counted the most pleasant of activities, but it is not the worst, either, and if you wish children of your own, it will be your duty to make him feel welcome in your bed."

"But..." Charlotte said, her brow furrowed. "But, how do I do that?"

"Hide those willful tendencies and keep a smile on your face no matter what he does." Her hands swiftly braided her daughter's hair, half-successfully tempering a glower in the looking glass. "Never hinder him, for he will know what to do, and in no time at all, I will have grandchildren and your husband will have an heir."

"But Sally said—"

"As I say, Charlotte Amberly, do not listen to the ravings of chambermaids about your marital bed."

Bella looked up with a curious look and said, "But Uncle Howard is so kind. Does he not—"

"Isabella Rowan Smithson! Never, ever let me hear you speak of my husband so again! If some man decides to marry you, ugly as you are, then you may discuss the bedchamber, and only with him."

Bella's head dropped, and she muttered, "Yes, Aunt Minerva."

"Until then, you will keep a civil tongue and act as though a virtuous girl could come from my accursed brother's loins. Charlotte, suffice it to say, you have a duty to your husband, and you will fulfill it without argument. Now then, off to bed with both of you."

Sneaking down the hall in the middle of the night reminded her of her escape from Brittlestep Manor with Alexan—Lord Firthley, though hopefully, this time, she would not rouse her brother. The odds, however, were against her, as her mother had assigned Ale —Lord Firthley a bedroom directly across the hall, and Hugh would wake at a pin drop.

When she reached Lord Firthley's bedchamber door, a faint light still glowed under the door, and her brother's nighttime candle had burned out, so he was fast asleep. She scratched her fingernail against the wooden door. If her brother woke, she hoped he would think it one of the mice that so terrified him and stay out of the hallway.

With no response, she scratched a bit louder, and finally, the third time, risked the quietest of taps with the tip of one finger. At last, footsteps crossed the room, and the door creaked open.

Charlotte choked.

His chest was entirely bare, covered with a mat of black curls she was almost compelled to touch. The top buttons of the fall of his trousers had been unfastened, pants hanging from his hips, feet bare. He might as well be naked.

She stood, mouth gaping, until he jumped back behind the door, only his face visible through the crack.

Staring over her shoulder, not at her dressing gown, he hissed, "Miss Amberly, what are you doing here?"

"I must speak to you."

"You cannot mean to come into my room?"

Her mouth dropped. "Of course not. Meet me in the library in five minutes."

"A darkened library is no better. Why?"

"Because if we stay here, Hugh will wake and call out for my father, and you do not want that."

He sighed and ran his fingers through his mussed hair, Charlotte watching every motion of the now-visible, muscular arm. When he noticed her looking, he twisted his arm back from the habitual gesture, hiding himself, once again, behind the door.

"Very well, but this is an awful idea."

She barely heard him, having already scooted down the hall.

Ten minutes later, fully dressed, including a cravat, gloves, and boots, Lord Firthley was still running his fingers through his hair as though keeping whatever he wished he could say from flying out of his head.

"Do not be ridiculous, Charlotte. We will be married in the morning if I have to set a footman to guard your door."

"I will not. You can tie me up and carry me to the church and threaten me with a hot poker, but you cannot force me to speak vows. Not when you don't love me and never will. Not when you are only doing this out of some misguided sense of honor."

"Honor?" His head tilted as he took in her dressing gown, no longer limiting his perusal to her face. "I am not sure honor is the word for my intentions, my dear."

Alexander, sidled closer, removing his gloves, a look in his eye she had never seen, but which made her stomach do a strange flip-flop.

"I've fought a duel at your request and won it without killing the despicable cur, saving you from ruin and your cousin from... from whatever ill fate it is you refuse to tell me. I've lied to your father as long as I could possibly manage it. I've helped you escape an unwelcome marriage. And I've offered for you to keep you safe from a villainous fiend. What more must I do to convince you of the sincerity of my affections?" He tucked a crooked finger under her chin so she could see nothing but his endearing smile.

She stepped back, and he stepped forward. Then another step. Then another. Her back hit a built-in shelf of books, and she chirruped. One of his hands rose and landed on the wall above her shoulder, the other graced her cheek, rubbing an oddly calloused thumb across her smooth skin. Leaning in, his elbow grazing the wall, he placed a soft kiss on her jawbone.

"What are...?" She trailed off when his lips moved to the side of her throat, tongue tip teasing her skin.

"How can you know if you wish to marry me when you don't even know if you enjoy my kisses?" he whispered in her ear.

Her whole body shivered, but she managed, "Kisses are... irrelevant..."

"Oh, no, my sweet. Kisses will never be irrelevant." With that, he took her chin between his finger and thumb and gently placed his lips over hers.

She tried to speak, to object, and he brushed his tongue along her upper lip. Her words caught in her throat, if she had any at all, and her body began to tremble like she was caught in a snow-storm in her chemise. He slanted his mouth to a more effective angle—good Heavens, was it effective—and let loose her chin to wrap his arm about her waist.

Dragging her closer, his tongue coaxed hers into a dance of sorts, a waltz, where her need to always win was subsumed in the pleasure of the caress. His other hand wandering into the hair at the nape of her neck, she felt him loosen her braid, strands of black caressing her shoulders, tangling around his fingers. When he tugged her head back and his tongue drifted along the column of her throat, she moaned. When he left soft, open-mouthed kisses along her collarbone, she whimpered. She reached her hand up to touch his chest, and when she did, it was as though lightning ran from his muscled form down her arm and into areas of her body better left unsaid.

"My mother said—"

"Shh, shh, never speak of her again while I am kissing you." He enforced his request by giving her no chance to speak further. The groaning she couldn't stop rumbled deep in her throat, increasing in volume with the progress of his hand from hip, to waist to—oh, Lord! His hand surrounded the globe of her breast, thumb brushing across her nipple as delicately as it had across her cheek, forcing her body to arch against him.

"Do you wish me to continue, my sweet?"

"Oh, yes, oh... please..."

He stepped back, holding her steady against the row of books. "Then you shall have to meet me at the altar in the morning."

She blinked in the candlelight, disoriented. "What?"

His sardonic grin was more than a little smug. "By nightfall tomorrow, I will finish what I've started, but not until you are well and truly my wife."

"But—"

He straightened her dressing gown, tied the sash tightly, and offered his arm. "Will I escort you back to your bedchamber now? You should sleep, for it will be a long day tomorrow."

She narrowed her eyes at him. "You horrible man. You meant to do that, to get me to... and then stop. You are a.... a...."

"Horrible man." He grinned.

"Yes!"

"Nevertheless," he murmured against her ear, "I will not show you the rest until you are mine. And there is oh, so much more."

He tucked her hand under his elbow and walked her on shaking legs to the door to her chamber. Pulling her against him for one last kiss, he whispered, "You set me aflame, Charlotte Amberly. It has been so since the first night, when I saw you eavesdropping on the stairway. Tomorrow night, I will give you all, and I swear, you will be the happiest of wives all our days. I cannot force you to speak vows, but your refusal will leave me hollow. Please do not disappoint me so, my dear."

The lightest touch of his fingertip to her cheek set her heart beating like a war drum, tremors of both mutiny and surrender crashing through her veins. He left her standing, shoulders against the door, staring at his back as he walked away down the hall.

CHAPTER FIFTEEN

B ella woke to sobbing from behind the connecting door to Charlotte's suite. If the silly chit did not soon make up her mind to marry the man she clearly wanted, she would send Bella mad. But Charlotte had always been like a barn cat going after a lion. No matter how bad the idea, she would scratch away at it until she won her point—or was flattened under someone's larger paw.

Bella pushed the door open.

"Charlotte? Are you injured? Is something amiss?" *Buffle-brained cow.* The only thing injured was Charlotte's pride and the only thing amiss, her desire to do things her own way.

Bella sat on the edge of the bed, stroking her cousin's hair as she sobbed into her pillow. "I know, dearest, it's too much, too fast. But it will all be over by this time tomorrow, and soon enough, you will be mistress of Lord Firthley's marquessate, chatelaine to four separate estates."

Charlotte's sobbing slowed, and she shifted the pillow.

"By nuncheon tomorrow, you will be wealthier than your father and outrank your mother forevermore."

She sniffled and shrugged.

"And you will never have to do another thing she says."

Charlotte turned over, scrubbing her face clean of tears on the sleeve of her nightrail. "But..."

"Yes?"

"But what if... what if..." She turned her head and mumbled into her pillow, "What if he doesn't love me?"

Bella giggled and slipped the pillow from under Charlotte's head. "What if he doesn't? Do you love him?"

"Well... no... not... I mean, perhaps I might..."

Bella hit her, none too gently, with the pillow. "You don't need to love him, Charlotte. He is kind and handsome and makes you laugh—don't deny it. He will make you a fine husband, and you will be a wonderful wife. You have wanted to be married since the first time you saw a bride."

Charlotte piled up pillows against the headboard. "What if he is the wrong husband for me? What if I might find someone perfect, if only I waited?"

Bella picked at the embroidery on the bedclothes. "Can you wait, with my brother doing his best to destroy you?"

Charlotte paused, but eventually said, "No, I don't suppose I can."

Taking up the same position she always had when the two girls kept each other awake into the wee hours, Bella crossed her legs and sat at the end of the bed, her back against the post.

"Have you met some other gentleman who might offer for you?"

Charlotte sat up, tucking her legs underneath her, back against the headboard. "No, but I've only been out for a few weeks, and there were several prospects who might—"

Bella tossed the bolster across the bed at Charlotte. "Who are they, then, these paragons who might come up to scratch if only you gave them long enough to do your bidding?"

"Well..." Charlotte began counting on her fingers. "Lord Melby said my hair is like midnight and my eyes like the stars. He said he could write a sonnet about me."

Bella snorted, "Did he write one? And has he somehow replenished his family's lost wealth by the writing of poetry?"

Charlotte huffed and bent her index finger, going on to the next. "The Earl of Chastain tried to take two dances at the Lindley ball. I had to be quite forceful."

"So you would marry a man who wishes to bend you to his will, in order to escape the same?"

"Well, no... but he—"

"Has three children and a tumble-down estate in Scotland with a roof that needs fixing with your dowry."

Narrowing her eyes, Charlotte ticked off another finger. "Viscount Ferrinday said—"

Bella sat up straight. "If you say you would marry Viscount Ferrinday, I will deliver you to the chapel tomorrow myself."

"What is so wrong with him?"

"He is one of the... he is..." she finished in a strangled whisper, "He is *friends* with John and Jeremy."

Charlotte's face went white, and she dropped the finger into her fist. "The Duke of Ordnay came to call twice."

Bella's giggles filled the room. "The Duke of Ordnay is older than Lord Firthley's grandfather, whom you ran away to avoid. Come, Charlotte. You cannot think of one good reason not to marry Lord Firthley, nor should you. He has proved himself each and every time you have tested him—" She held up one finger. "Do not tell me you haven't tested him, for I have seen it myself."

Bella began ticking off her own fingers: "He helped you run from Evercreech. He lied to your parents without being asked. He kept your secret when he could have ruined you. He offered for you when Jeremy was your only other choice. He pinked my brother in a duel to save both of us from the next round of

Smithson scheming. And all without destroying the last shreds of your good name." She arranged the blanket to cover her bare feet. "No, my dear, dimwitted cousin. He is the man for you. There is no doubt of that."

Charlotte blushed bright red, and when she started working her finger through a small tear in the counterpane, Bella seized her hand. "What is it? You are smiling."

"It's just... well... only, I met him in the library a half-hour past."

Bella's hand covered her mouth to hold in the gasp, and her eyes went wide as dinner plates. "No," she said with a morbid fascination. "Did he ruin you utterly?"

"No! The horrid man."

Bella giggled.

"I mean... that's not what I meant..." Charlotte looked at the window on the side of the room. "Only he kissed me and it was... it was quite... well... Mother didn't say it would be like..." she whispered, "like *that!*"

"Like what?" Bella was now fascinated.

"I can't describe it, really... just... it was... decadent... like sliding into a cool pond on a hot day. And he touched my..." She gestured to her chest.

"No! He didn't! Charlotte!"

"I don't see what is so wrong with it. We are to be married tomorrow, and it isn't as though he did... whatever husbands do."

"Are you certain?"

"I expect I am, since he still had his gloves and cravat on!"

"Is that all?" Bella snickered.

"No, that is not all." Charlotte threw the bolster back at her cousin. "Fully clothed. All but a hat and cane. And as I say," her nose turned up, "I will be his wife in the morning, so I see nothing wrong in a few kisses."

Bella took Charlotte's hand and squeezed it. "Nor do I, darling."

Finally, Charlotte had relented and let herself win.

"Now, it will be cock's crow in no time, and you will have circles beneath your eyes if you do not sleep."

Charlotte nodded, tucking her feet back under the bedclothes, and Bella crossed the room to the connecting door.

"Bella?"

"Yes?"

"Thank you."

Bella blew her a kiss and skittered through the door, before Charlotte could talk herself out of being sensible again.

CHAPTER SIXTEEN

The next day...

"I must speak to him, Mother!"

"He cannot see you before the wedding, and you may not go roaming around the halls in this expensive gown."

Charlotte's gown of cloth-of-silver was among the simplest she had ever owned, but for the pearls at the hem and along the bust line, and the train that reached four feet behind her. The silver and pearl tiara that had belonged to her great-grandmother was the inspiration for the dress and the oldest, most valuable piece of jewelry her mother owned—or rather, Charlotte owned, for her father had given it to her as a wedding gift, a tradition her mother had been loath to uphold.

Regardless of seemliness, Charlotte would soon only have to obey her husband, and she fully planned to never do anything her mother said again. Beginning with a convention she found inconvenient. Seeing the matching, resolute mother-and-daughter chins, Bella stepped up and intervened. "I will bring him here, so you need not risk the gown, and your maid can move the dressing screen across the doorway to my chamber, so he cannot see you."

Charlotte jumped up and down and kissed Bella on the cheek. "Yes! That is exactly what we must do." While Bella slipped out the door and Lady Effingale's abigail began shifting the screen, the bride turned her back on her mother and began poking at her coiffure and adjusting her dress.

In only a few minutes, she heard the door to Bella's bedchamber open and demanded her mother leave the vicinity in the most imperious "I-will-be-a-marchioness-in-less-than-two-hours" voice she could muster. Charlotte could hear Bella in the hallway, reassuring Lady Effingale that Lord Firthley was a gentleman and Charlotte too smart to allow him liberties.

"Charlotte, what is it? Are you quite well?" The strain in his voice evidenced his fear she would jilt him in these final moments.

"Yes, yes, I am perfectly well. It's only..." She twisted a button on her sleeve.

"Yes?"

"Do you..." She slipped it in and out of the loop. "I am afraid you..."

"What are you afraid of, my sweet?"

She shoved the words out of her mouth before she could regret saying them. "*Iamafraidyouwillneverloveme.*"

The silence from the other side of the screen caused tears to well up in her eyes, and she unbuttoned the sleeve and began to remove the tiara. In a moment, however, he pushed the screen aside and entered the room.

His fingertips under her chin closed her dropped open mouth, and his thumb caressed her bottom lip. "I will not observe a silly custom when my bride is concerned for my faith-fulness." His hands moved to her shoulders, and he looked down into her eyes.

"Do you love me?" he asked, with more serious a countenance than she had yet seen.

She swallowed hard and tipped her head. "I hadn't... I mean... that is to say..."

"You do not. Of course you do not, only days after making my acquaintance. Nor can I say I feel as deep an emotion as love."

The tremble of her lips sent a tear down her cheek. "But... but what if we... what if we never do?"

He kissed her on the forehead and wrapped his arms about her shoulders, pulling her tiara-laden head to his chest. Stroking her hair, he answered, "My sweet, I am fascinated by you. Your adventurous spirit, your charm, your smiles. I wish nothing more than to see your face at my table each morning and in my bed each night. This may not be love, my darling, but it is as close an approximation as I have ever known.

"In truth, I am equally afraid you will not learn to love me, but we must have faith our union will be satisfying for us both. For I will not leave you to that reprobate, Smithson, nor the tender mercies of the *ton*. That, my dear, I cannot do, and if that is not proof of... something... I do not know what is."

"I find the fact you do not love me oddly reassuring." Pushing at his chest, she pouted up at him. "But what if it is *not* satisfying? What if you leave me in the country and find a mistress in Town and never speak to me but to get an heir?"

"Do I speak to you now, and at least mildly entertain you?"

"Yes."

"Will you follow me to Town and force your way into my house at gunpoint should I attempt to leave you at one of my country estates?"

"Yes."

"Will you box my ears should I engage a mistress?"

"Yes."

"Do you truly think me a horrible, despicable man?"

She blushed and smiled at his cravat. "No."

"Well, then, we will both have to be satisfied with that. I expect, in time, we will grow much fonder of each other than we can imagine now. And, yes, it may come to love."

She sighed against his shirtfront and twisted her finger around his waistcoat button. "Will you... will you do that... what you did last night?"

Placing a gentle kiss on the top of her head, he said, a husky rasp in his voice, "I will. As soon as practical and as often as possible, and I promise that part of our marriage will always be satisfying to both of us."

She startled herself by giggling, and he asked, "Might I go finish preparing myself to meet you at St. George's in..." He removed his watch his pocket. "Eighty-seven minutes?"

She nodded, but before he left, he gave her another of the kisses he had shown her twelve hours earlier. By the time he finished, her knees were weak, and she had only eighty-one minutes to wait.

CHAPTER SEVENTEEN

Later that night...

Charlotte's knee would not stop bouncing under her nightrail and dressing gown. Seated on a loveseat in her unfamiliar new bedchamber, in this unfamiliar new town house far enough away from her parents' home to warrant a carriage ride, she had already spilled half a glass of sherry on herself and had to change, hoping her new husband wouldn't come into the room while she was unclothed. Or perhaps hoping he would.

Bother! If he would only put away whatever he was doing that was so much more important than bedding his wife the first time, this would already be finished, and she might be sleeping soundly. Then he could do whatever he wanted in his study all night long, and it wouldn't trouble her a bit. If only he would hurry!

Tiptoeing over to the door connecting their suites, she set her ear against the wood, listening for any noises that would indicate he was there, waiting, maybe as nervous as she. Nothing but silence. She knelt down on one knee to peer through the keyhole, but all was dark. Perhaps he had gone right to sleep. Perhaps he didn't mean to consummate their marriage at all. Perhaps he would—

"Ahem," she heard from the hall. There he stood, in shirt-sleeves and an untied cravat, looking more sinfully handsome than any man had a right to after a long, nerve-racking day. She scrambled to her feet, unable to say a word in the face of his snickering, sputtering, stifled amusement. When she narrowed her eyes, he finally allowed the laughter to break free.

"Charlotte, my sweet, if you are so anxious for me to attend you, I give you leave to seek me out in any room of the house."

"No! I mean..." She gathered her dignity, turning her nose up into the air, wrapping her dressing gown more tightly around her waist. "You are at perfect liberty to do anything you like in your own home."

The smile didn't leave his face, but the flavor changed from mirth to something gentler, kinder. He stepped across the room and cradled her face in his hands. "It is cruel of me to laugh, my dearest. I simply never imagined I might find my wife peeking through the keyhole into my bedchamber. There is no lock on the door. I can have it repaired if you'd like, but in truth, you are at *perfect liberty* to come to my rooms any time you like." Placing a kiss on the top of her head, he leaned her cheek onto his shoulder and murmured, "I would very much like it if you did."

Charlotte's indrawn breath caught, turning to a fit of coughing that had her bent at the waist, trying to clear her throat for breathing. Guiding her gently, her new husband sat her down on the same loveseat, then poured tea from the pot she had abandoned for the sherry while she waited. It was lukewarm, but silenced her choking.

As she sipped, he knelt down to ensure she recovered.

"Are you all right, my dear? Can you breathe properly now?" She nodded, sure she was now red-faced, trying to subtly ensure her lower lip wasn't covered in tea and spittle. She thought she might die of the humiliation. Drooling like an infant; it wasn't to be borne.

He removed the cravat from around his neck, using it to wipe her mouth and chin. "Husbands must be of some use, after all." Tucking the neckcloth away, he continued, "And as to that, I believe I recall your intent in running away was to ensure you had your Season, was it not?"

She looked down at the floor and silently nodded.

"And by our precipitate marriage, you will be denied all but the first few weeks of parties."

She repeated herself without words, adding a scowl.

"Your mother has informed me she expects me to take you to the country immediately to avoid any scandal, and your parents will remove with Bella to Brittlestep Manor in two days' time, for that selfsame purpose."

A melancholy nod once more.

"Are you concerned for scandal?"

She looked up. One shoulder shrugged; she was unwilling to commit to an unknown course.

"I thought not," he said, tweaking her nose, "after placing your reputation, and mine, in grave danger, purely for the privilege of bowing before the queen." His sweet smile belied any ill will he might hold. "I've received the Writ of Summons to take my grandfather's seat in Parliament. For the moment, no one knows my politics, so I can expect some deference until the lords decide whether to curry favor, and I've married you to scrub your reputation clean. If the gossip does not concern you, I am not averse to remaining, allowing you your parties. If you can stand to be half of the Filthy Firthleys for a time."

She threw herself at him, oversetting his balance, leaving him sprawled on his backside, laughing. Her arms wound around his neck like tentacles.

"Oh, thank you, Lord F—" Taking in his ignoble position, and her own, she sat back abruptly, shoulders against the seat of the sofa, hand on his knee. His eyes twinkling at her in the way she so loved, she amended, "Alexander."

Suddenly serious, he leaned across her lap to kiss her. "Much better."

"It is so kind of you to—" Her nervous chitter-chatter was swallowed up as his lips met hers. It became a moan when his tongue slid along her lower lip. Opening her mouth just slightly to grant him access, and allowing his hand in her long hair to gently maneuver her onto her back on the carpet before the fireplace, she couldn't help but whimper. The shivers his fingers induced pulsed in every area of her body, especially the unmentionable parts.

She tried to pull him closer, but he resisted, saying, "Oh, no, my sweet. We have all night, and I intend to use every minute."

Through lust-fogged sight, she took in his smug smile. "Every... it lasts all night?"

"It does when you are with me," he whispered in her ear. "Where you will wish to be forevermore."

Without another word, she grasped his hair between her fingers and pulled him closer for another kiss, using every ounce of her new-found passion to ensure he never let her go.

The End

THANKS FOR READING!

If you liked *'Tis Her Season*, please help others find books they will love by leaving a review wherever you bought the book.

For the first chapter of the other *Sailing Home* series books, keep reading.

ABOUT THE AUTHOR

Mari A. Christie has been a professional writer, editor, and designer for almost 40 years. Published in dozens of nonfiction and poetry periodicals since 1987, she began writing mainstream historical fiction in 2009 and Regency romance in 2013. In all genres, she creates deeply scarred characters in uncommon circumstances who overcome self-imposed barriers to reach their full potential. She is a member of the Paper Lantern Writers and the Historical Novel Society.

Author Website: www.MariAnneChristie.com

BY MARI A. CHRISTIE

HISTORICAL ROMANCE

Royal Regard

When Bella Holsworthy returns to London after fifteen years roaming the globe, she faces unwelcome attentions from two wicked noblemen, the ton's spiteful censure, and the bitter realities of a woman alone in England.

'Tis Her Season: A Royal Regard prequel novella

Charlotte Amberly gives back a Christmas gift from her intended—the ring—then hares off to London to take husband-hunting into her own hands. Will she let herself be caught?

Shipmate: A Royal Regard prequel novella

Bella Holsworthy's Happy-Ever-After in Royal Regard had its origins in a Happier-Than-She-Expected with her first husband, who gave her the confidence to steady her sea legs, take her life by the helm, and command her own voice, empowering a shy, young girl to grow into one of King George IV's trusted advisors.

A Rose Renamed: A Royal Regard prequel novella

(coming Spring 2026)

Major John Smythe returns from Waterloo a broken man, determined to stay one step ahead of his former life, but when he meets Rose Allen, the sins of his past must be confronted, for without her, he has no hope for a future

HISTORICAL FICTION

Blind Tribute

Every newspaper editor owes tribute to the devil; Harry Wentworth's bill just came due.

SHORT HISTORICAL FICTION FROM THE PAPER LANTERN WRITERS

Unlocked

Editor and contributor

"Threadbare Linens"

Beneath a Midwinter Moon

Editor and contributor

"Long Winter"

Destiny Comes Due

Editor and contributor

"Autumn Angel"

NON-FICTION

Brainstorm Your Book: Planning the Parts of You Next Novel

Brainstorm Your Book: Planning the Parts of You Next Novel is a hands-on, pen-to-paper, rubber-to-road workbook to help you generate ideas for all the elements of your next fiction book.

Crafting Stories from the Past: A How-To Guide for Writing Historical Fiction

Editor and contributor

Whether you are just starting your path into the past or are a seasoned multi-book historical fiction author, Paper Lantern Writers bring you tips, tricks, ideas, and resources you can use at every stage of your writing journey

ROYAL REGARD

When Bella Holsworthy returns to England after fifteen years roaming the globe with her husband, an elderly diplomat, she quickly finds herself in a place more perilous than any in her travels—the Court of King George IV. As the newly elevated Earl and Countess settle into an unfamiliar life in London, this shy, not-so-young lady faces wicked agendas, society's censure, and the realities of a woman soon to be alone in England.

Unaccustomed to the ways of the beau monde, she is disarmed and deceived by a dissolute duke and a noble French émigré with a silver tongue. Hindered by the meddling of her dying husband, not to mention the King himself, Bella must decide whether to choose one of her fascinating new suitors or the quiet country life she has searched the world to find.

Continue on to the first chapter.

ROYAL REGARD

CHAPTER ONE

1820: London, England

Teeth clenched against the wrong thing she was sure to say, shoulders cramped and stomach churning, Baroness Holsworthy smoothed down the tiers of ruffles on her borrowed dress, tapping her toe out of rhythm to the music. The stays she wore so infrequently, but would never abandon in London, dug into her waist like a fork into flummery.

Bella tried not to stare into the looking glasses lining the Almack's ballroom, hoping to appear insouciant, well above silly concerns of wardrobe and hairstyle, ignoring the sight of her lips trembling. However, this only left her to look at the overwhelming crowd of vexatious people, not just their harmless reflections.

She picked at the poorly fitting, delicate tulle floating around her body, a borrowed dress better suited to her prettier cousin Charlotte at age seventeen than either woman in their thirties. Wriggling her shoulders beneath the almost-adequate alterations Charlotte's maid had accomplished in the fifteen minutes allotted for the impossible task, Bella thoroughly regretted her spontaneous decision to call on her cousin so late in the day.

The music had already started for a *contredanse*, but she paid little attention to the dancers taking their places, distracted by the bright candlelight mirrored in the gilt trim along every wall. She stopped her toe drumming against the parquet floor; given her situation, there was no prospect of dancing, so it made no sense to engage even one foot with the music. Of course, the only other activity to engage in was gossip, from which she would be excluded by virtue of being the primary topic.

The aristocrats peering at her through quizzing glasses over the bannister of the upper floor set her heart trembling, so she turned the corner of her eye, her peripheral vision next caught by a grouping of at least half a dozen women, just outside her hearing, staring at her as they chattered behind their fans.

It seemed a fine moment to take in the frescos above the bas-relief mouldings, all pretty enough, but no masterpieces here. The sculpture might as well be plaster pasted onto the cheapest marble veneers, and the paintings could have been commissioned from any student at the Royal Academy. Having seen so many masterworks around the world, she could find nothing to keep her attention from wandering back to the echoes of guests in the wavy pier glass, which had been silvered poorly and was, if she looked closely, somewhat unclean.

She patted at her chignon, searching out loose tendrils of her stick-straight hair. Surely, it would be falling out of the tight ringlets by now, a style that made her face look a half-stone heavier and had no chance of surviving the heat of the crowds, no matter how chilly the spring evening outside the door. As suspected, loose strands were already sticking to the back of her neck above her nearly bared shoulders, and she grimaced, envisioning the sweaty mess in plain view of anyone behind her.

She sought her husband in the crush of bodies, mindful of her fluttering hands, but unable to quell them. Craning her neck, her nose wrinkled against too many colognes barely masking the smell of too many people. Her cousin, the Marchioness of Firthley, appeared at her side and snapped her fan across Bella's arm.

"You look like you have a palsy, Bella. Stop twitching. They will be along shortly."

Between her rigid carriage, the height of her coiffure of black curls, the steep heels of her dancing shoes, and the sleek velvet gown making her appear more slender than her figure allowed, Charlotte seemed to tower above Bella, though she wasn't more than an inch taller. Less than a year older, the unyielding lines of her proud visage added a decade to her show of superiority.

Bella reined in her movements, but continued to eye the throng. "I merely—" She crumpled a ruffle near her hip without noticing the fists she had formed.

"It was the only dress I had that could be altered."

Sighing, Bella capitulated, "You carry no blame for my dreadful silhouette."

Papa had always called her *sturdy*. Unfashionably square in form, with rather broad shoulders, her best feature lovely, long legs she had always wished she could use to her advantage. While Empire styles flattered her figure as much as clothing ever did, she had never fit comfortably into Charlotte's dresses, even with enough corseting to buckle her knees. These scores of ruffles made her look more like an Egyptian column than a woman.

Smiling more gently, Charlotte patted the pink mark the fan had made on Bella's forearm, reminding her cousin yet again, "Even after fifteen years, they are the same people they were when you left, and you are now a baroness with a goodly fortune and a husband distinguished in the diplomatic service. You may find you are made a countess before long. Alexander says four-to-one at White's." Charlotte's sharp eyes flashed, and she spoke from the side of her mouth. "Prepare to pretend you are civilized. You've been spotted."

Reflected in the silvery glass behind Charlotte, Bella's eyes widened in alarm, and beneath her unfashionably sun-warmed skin, her face paled. Pivoting, she insinuated herself behind Charlotte's right arm and ducked her head behind the princess sleeve of Charlotte's much lovelier gown.

Charlotte stepped away, leaving her no place to hide. "Lady Lannedae and Lady Yarley are coming this way, and I shall have to present you to the hostesses before long, or we will be summoned. It is miraculous I could secure vouchers without an interview."

"Only so Lady Jersey can be first to tell tales," Bella grumbled in a higher-pitched voice than she had meant, as she smoothed down the awful dress. Charlotte poked her fan at Bella's hand. "Stop it. You have to face the gossips sometime."

Charlotte and Bella both curtsied to the much older ladies, and Charlotte made the introductions: "Lady Yarley, Lady Lannadae, might I present my cousin, Lady Holsworthy?"

Both ladies sniffed, as though they hadn't come over specifically to speak to her. Lady Yarley's mouth puckered like she was sucking soured food from her teeth, and Lady Lannadae's eyes snapped as viciously as a hungry crocodile. They stood straighter than Bella's hair, elbows tucked into their sides, hands grasped tightly across their old-fashioned waistlines, identical but for color—one lady in mauve with grey trim and the other grey trimmed in mauve—both restraining themselves to the last vestiges of pretended courtesy.

Bella knew the role she had to play, no matter how unpleasant it might be. Her husband had always depended on her gracious behavior and deference toward anyone with whom he might do business, most especially men's wives. It was very nearly second nature, even in London, so she pasted on a simpering smile.

"Ladies, I am so pleased to meet you. It has been far too long since I have spoken to civilized people in the English tongue. Lady Lannadae, I must say the lace on your gown is lovelier than any I have seen, even in Brussels. I hope you might tell me where you found it."

Without so much as a how-do-you-do, Lady Yarley ripped into her subject as a wild dog into a cornered coney. "I've heard you and Lord Holsworthy have been in the most disreputable places—the Dark Continent, the Spanish New World—"

Lady Lannadae broke in, "The penal colonies!"

Eyeing her cohort coldly, Lady Yarley continued, "I cannot imagine any well-bred young lady surviving such a voyage."

Both of the women's eyes narrowed to exactly the same slits.

Bella's mouth twisted into a patently false depiction of continued civility. "The blizzards of Siberia, the monsoons of the Orient, the tropics of South America..." As the ladies leaned in, intolerance dripping from their rabid fangs, Bella abruptly decided to provide them fresh meat.

In a clear, uplifted voice, infused with the ice of a Russian winter, she continued: "Some places, one can hardly stand to wear any clothing at all. I have seen more natives *au naturel* than you might imagine exist on the planet."

Lady Lannadae sucked in a breath, nearly swooning.

Charlotte's voice took on a shrill tone as she laughed too loudly, "My cousin is such a goose. Of course, she is joking." Jabbing the fan into Bella's side, she whispered, "*Au naturel...* My heavens, Bella."

Lady Yarley spoke to fill her companion's shocked silence. "No lady of my acquaintance would stand for such immodesty."

"Given the choice of standing for it or being cut up and made into British-subject soup," Bella returned, "I learned to cope with the indiscretions of people who know no better. I like to think I was a civilizing influence."

Suddenly feeling her age and experience, Bella determined to hide neither.

"Of course, we haven't been without the trappings of civilization entirely. We've just spent the last half-year as guests of King Louis in Paris, though lavish apartments in the Tuileries Palace were not our standard fare. Most often it was riding astride on camels and bathing in river water under tents. When we had tents, of course. And the food! Rancid meat, offal, reptiles, insects; the retching alone might have killed me. And obviously, only by the grace of God have I made it back without being raped to death by hordes of barbarians."

Judging by the matching pinched looks of horror on their faces, if Lady Lannadae and Lady Yarley hadn't leaned against each other, they both might have fainted dead away on the Aubusson carpet. Charlotte fumbled in her reticule, presumably for smelling salts.

"It has been so lovely to meet you, ladies," Bella said crisply. "You must feel free to call. I will be receiving Monday and Thursday afternoons." Turning away from them, Bella once more sought her husband through the crowds in which she would soon be a social pariah. In that moment, she didn't give a whit, but was canny enough to know she would later.

Before the ladies could respond, even before Charlotte could voice the horror crossing her face, a man stepped up to introduce himself, ignoring the need to be presented, his lips turned up at Bella's pointed depictions.

"*Bonsoir*, ladies," he nodded briefly, but didn't bow, to each of them. All of the women curtsied, though Charlotte's face fell still and silent.

"I had hoped to gain an introduction to the celebrated Baroness Holsworthy." He bowed deeply and kissed Bella's hand before she offered. "I have heard you are the most fascinating creature to grace our shores in a century."

Charlotte grimaced as she made the presentation: "Lady Holsworthy, may I present Adolphe Fouret, Monsieur le Duc de Malbourne?"

His dark hair was cut short, slicked back with pomade from a widow's peak, highlighting eyes and brows black as coal and deep as a quarry. High cheekbones and a hawk-like Gallic nose spoke of an aristocratic bloodline, and flawlessly tailored evening clothes showed a likely fortune to perfection, every inch in black but for his pave-diamond *fleur-de-lys* cravat pin, emblematic of the French monarchy. A lifetime of haughtiness preceded him, thicker than the scent of bergamot wafting from his hair.

"*Enchantée, Monseigneur,*" Bella said in his native language. "Are you enjoying the party?"

"But of course, you speak French," he observed in English, "and with a perfect accent."

"*Mais oui.* How could I entertain in Paris otherwise?"

Lord Malbourne chuckled and his smile slid like a fingertip up her arm. He continued the exchange in French, excluding the other women by posture, if not conversation.

"I hope you will indulge me one day soon with your impressions of Paris. It has been more than thirty years since I last stood on French soil, almost too young to be called a man."

Bella considered his probable age and took in his still youthful appearance: hair only slightly silvered at the temples, face barely lined, spine straight and unyielding. His frame was still powerful and athletic, more like a man twenty years younger. More like a man who might attract a woman her age.

Lady Yarley and Lady Lannadae watched closely, one with eyes on her, the other staring at the duke, switching with every utterance. Realizing she had been considering his body much longer than she should, Bella shook her head and cleared her throat to return to the present moment.

"I would be pleased to engage in such discourse, Your Grace, but I am afraid you will find my impressions weigh heavily toward *le Jardin des Tuileries* and *le Musée du Louvre*, not intrigues at Court."

"Of course," he agreed, shoulders held straighter once he noticed she was looking. "But I have heard from across the water that you are a most original hostess and patroness of the arts. Your small suppers and *soirées musicales* are very nearly legend. I will look forward to dancing with you this evening, if you will permit." His lips twitched. "Perhaps you will share some tales of your travels. I have heard they are *très amusants*."

"You will have to ask my husband, Your Grace, for I shan't dance at all without his accord."

It was her customary answer in any unfamiliar ballroom, until she could discern the undercurrents of the event, and until Myron advised on any men whom she needed to impress with her flawless dancing and charming gentility. Once finished with that chore, she could retire to a seat along the wall.

Lady Yarley snapped, "It is a wonder your husband—"

"I certainly understand," Lord Malbourne agreed, dismissing Lady Yarley with his eyes. "Although I shall be bereft should he refuse. If you will forgive, I have other business to attend, but will search you out as soon as I might speak to Lord Holsworthy." Bella felt her color rise as he bent over her hand again; she dared not look at the elderly women who were sure to pass on this even-better gossip. "Until then, *ma chère*."

Hot, restless unease travelled down her neck; her cheeks flamed when she felt it spread to the low *décolletage* of the loathsome dress, and then watched Malbourne's eyes follow. His lips turned up in a barely perceptible leer—a subtle, momentary expression of raw desire and innate carnal authority somehow even more French than his conversation.

His nod both acknowledged and dismissed everyone in the vicinity but Bella, from whom he would not look away. Dropping her gaze to the floor, her eyes swept the corners of the room, searching an escape from his scrutiny. Finally, he snapped his heels together and backed into the crowd.

Before she could take up the conversation again, Lady Lannadae and Lady Yarley excused themselves, presumably to tell everyone in London that the Duke of Malbourne had just called her 'dear.'

"Bella!" Charlotte snapped. "That was awful! You can't just talk about *naked barbarians* at Almack's."

"I'll speak of anything I like to such horrible old cats. They are lucky I didn't come here tonight in trousers with a dagger and pistol in my belt." Bella said, tossing her head, feeling more ringlets fall out of their pins. "They had no liking for me fifteen years ago, nor I them." Her voice revealed a bit more bravado than good for her. "Myron is still a *parvenu*, and I am the daughter of a disgraced baronet. We wouldn't even have Strangers' Tickets if not for you."

"Myron has the king's confidence, Countess Peagoose, and you have Myron's. As long as you both stay in Prinny's favor, you can dine out among the social set forever."

"To my infinite dismay."

Bella had never aspired to be part of the social whirl. Her childhood had been spent entirely on Charlotte's father's estate in Somerset. Charlotte, the viscount's daughter, resided in the sixty-room manor house. Bella lived with her destitute father and brothers in a run-down cottage on the outskirts of her uncle's land: three rooms above, three below.

With no dowry to speak of, no firm foothold in the landed gentry, and no semblance of a pretty face, it was only by the sponsorship of her cousin and aunt that she had any prospects at all. If not for them, Bella would have been married to a country squire or a vicar with low expectations—or more likely, never married at all. She couldn't imagine what machinations must have been required to gain her admittance to these exclusive assembly rooms.

"I have no wish to be a countess, and it is much simpler to act the baroness while wearing one's own clothes."

"It couldn't be helped," Charlotte said. "It is not my fault you were robbed. I cannot imagine why you stayed at the Blue Bear. Everyone knows—"

"I am now well aware what everyone knows."

Bella wished she and her husband had never stopped at the horrible roadside inn. They had woken to find a sneak thief had stolen the night's receipts from the innkeeper and money and valuables from every traveler, including the Holsworthy's luggage and their coach from the stables.

The theft had been a real blow. They had lost her only child's christening gown, a gift from Charlotte that had never been used; Myron's war medals from the rebellion in the American colonies; the miniatures that were the only remembrances she had of her family; and the elegant Parisian gown she had intended to wear to her first party in London.

Still, she could only find fault with Charlotte for forcing her to be here, not for her own unreasonable fear. She wished she had stayed at home, curled up with a novel in the library.

"We could have waited to attend a party. We haven't settled into the house yet, and the trip wearied my husband more than he will admit. I must be concerned for his health."

"Nonsense. Myron is as spry as ever."

Bella's lips compressed into a thin line; Charlotte's constant references to the thirty-two-year age difference had started even before she married him, and only Bella knew how dangerously ill Myron had been on the trip back to England. Even Myron pretended he had no notion.

"You have been here more than a week without attending any

parties," Charlotte nagged, "and you would never present yourself anywhere unless forced to it."

"I have become quite adept at parties, and in any case, common courtesy would have forced the issue soon enough. It is simply easier to feel elegant and refined in the company of people with every reason to be kind to a man and his wife on His Majesty's business. Myron has more influence in Ceylon or Barbados or Sierra Leone than in London, and no one likes a bookish girl in England." Bella bit her lip. "I know my place, Charlotte. I just would have preferred to face the ordeal in the dress I had made for the occasion."

"You look quite handsome," Charlotte argued. "Your hair is straight as a plumb line, but the color is brilliant as ever, not even a trace of grey." Charlotte smoothed it in the front. "And you have finally grown into your face."

Bella's nerves fled with a cynical laugh and an impudent curtsey. "I am ever so grateful for the backhanded compliments, Your Ladyship." A habitual, playful disparagement raked over her cousin. "I can be as handsome as I want since I caught and kept a husband, and I am offended you discount my scintillating conversation after I have worked so hard at it all this time. The Governor-General of British India finds me fascinating."

"And no doubt the commandant of the penal colonies."

"The title you are looking for is Governor of New South Wales, and yes, Governor Macquarie and Myron have been acquainted for many years, beginning in India, and his wife, Elizabeth, and I were quite bosom friends both times we were in the Antipodes. She is the one whose care of the natives—"

She broke off when Charlotte held her hand out. "I beg you not continue about natives."

To distract Charlotte from further comment, and put an end to any argument, she inclined her head toward Malbourne, murmuring, "He is very handsome."

Across the room, he was under siege by a young lady on the shelf at two-and-twenty, scandalously dressed in near-translucent silver muslin, whom, it seemed, had been pushed into the inappropriate pursuit by an ever-vigilant mother trying to find a way to compromise her daughter.

Charlotte spoke even more quietly than her cousin. "Leave off any interest in Lord Malbourne. He's *French*, as though you need to know any more. You must not let him flirt so."

"Keeping a Frenchman from flirting is like keeping a snake from a mongoose." At Charlotte's raised eyebrow, Bella explained with a half-smile, "The mongoose might win, but most likely, the snake will slither away to try again."

"Why is he here?" Bella asked when Charlotte stopped giggling. "I know the war is over, but I confess I thought London hostesses would be fighting yet. And why 'Lord?' Is he not a duke?"

"He is a *French* duke," Charlotte said, as though it were explanation for any rudeness she cared to inflict, "though he has been in England most of his life," Charlotte started, clearly enthralled by the prospect of passing on delicious tittle-tattle. "You may have met him when—"

Bella shook her head.

"Well, you were only in London a few weeks. His late wife inherited land near Dover, and he took possession just before the Revolution. I heard he left her to die by guillotine, but Alexander says she was taken in childbed."

"Does Alexander know everything about everyone?"

"Yes. Now, hush, or I won't pass on what he's told me." Bella closed her mouth before Charlotte made good her threat. "He entertained King Louis at his manor house during the exile, and it's said he loaned King George half a million pounds toward the war debt, but that is probably a lie. Everyone knows he lost all his money when he ran from the rabble in Paris. Now that the

Little Corporal has been deposed, *Monsieur le Duc* is making the rounds of London again, pretending to be better than he is. They say he is looking for a wife, but he won't pay attention to any one girl."

"Why did a pedigreed *émigré* not return to France when—"

Before Bella could complete her question, their husbands joined them at last. Alexander Marloughe, Marquess of Firthley, moderated his lengthy stride to match Bella's spouse, who tottered on a cane, supporting a gouty leg and declining state of frailty, both of which had precipitated their return to England.

When Alexander held out his arm to provide a steadying hand, the elderly man stumbled slightly to the side to avoid it. Myron Clewes, Baron Holsworthy, could be a stubborn man when he so chose. Stepping to his side, Bella slipped her arm through her husband's, in order that he might lean on her surreptitiously, an inconspicuous position both comfortable and well established.

After many years of salt winds and tropical suns, they were both unfashionably tanned. For her part, Bella welcomed it, for it helped to hide the lines she was starting to see in her mirror, although one more mark against her in polite society. On Myron, the lines were years past hiding, as was his thinning shock of white hair, twice as bright just by proximity to his darkened face.

"My dear, I am so sorry to have kept you waiting," Myron said, grasping Bella's arm more tightly than usual. "Was that Malbourne I saw?"

"Yes." Bella was taken aback. "You know him?"

Myron's lips were suddenly thinner, his face almost ashen. "I know of him, and will not allow his attentions toward my wife."

"Of course, husband," she said, bowing her head to the chastisement, letting any irritation drift into the crosscurrents of rumor and innuendo. Myron would entertain her thoughts, opinions, observations, questions, or arguments on any topic she chose—at home. In public, she always agreed with him.

"He's right, Bella," Alexander said. "Slippery man, that. Not good *ton*."

"'Good *ton*,'" Bella pronounced, "is a contradiction in terms."

Alexander didn't disagree, only turned to his wife, saying, "I wish you wouldn't force me to Almack's, Charlotte. Knee breeches are as bad as a ball gown." He shifted in his clothes, pulling at his cravat until it was drawn askew. With his hair tied and powdered in the manner of several older, more influential members of Parliament, and attired in formal black breeches, clocked cream stockings and a coat of black superfine, he appeared closer to Myron's age, a quarter-century beyond his one-and-forty. He had not yet matured, however, into the same sense of quiet dignity.

Charlotte smiled and adjusted his collar. "Don't be ridiculous, my love. You are most distinguished and would look frightful in a frock. You haven't the figure for it," she laughed, continuing, "You will be pleased to know if Bella has her way, we shall be removed from the guest list entirely before the evening is out. *Naked savages*, indeed. Myron, it is scandalous you give her license to throw indecent stories around like brickbats."

Myron patted his wife's hand. "She needs no license from me. She is a grown woman, perfectly capable of speaking her own mind." Myron inclined his head toward Charlotte's mutinous expression in a half-conciliatory gesture. "Though I'm sure you understand the way of things in London much better than I."

Irritated at being discussed as though she weren't present, Bella spoke just as the music stopped: "I don't give a tuppenny damn for the way of things in London!" Her voice carried much further than she had intended, and a collective gasp rose from everyone in hearing distance, followed by a buzz of denigration that spread across the room like a wave across water.

Charlotte snapped her fan much harder on Bella's hand, her mouth opening and closing, choking on the words to express her outrage. Lips twitching, Alexander and Myron covered their amusement with observations about the orchestra's rapidly chosen next selection, a polka.

"You will kindly moderate your language, or I will take you home at once," Charlotte hissed, rounding on the gentlemen. "And you two! Encouraging her!"

"I am not a child to be sent to my room without supper, Charlotte," Bella snapped. "I have a voucher, so I will be staying." She would rather dine on rotten meat than endure another hour at Almack's, but a breakfast of ground glass was preferable to yielding to Charlotte.

"If anyone is to send her to her room without supper, my dear Lady Firthley, it will be me." Myron spoke gently, in the tone he always used to forestall further argument. Bella's coy smirk sent a message to him that shut out everyone else in the room without being at all inappropriate.

Charlotte snapped, "I might think you would encourage her to act like a proper wife, before it gets back to the king that she is still an incurable hoyden."

"I daresay you might think so," Myron answered, "but I assure you, His Majesty is well aware she is a hoyden. He has come to see it as a great asset." Bella flushed at this encomium and lowered her eyes under Myron's indulgent smile. "He has never failed to ask after her, and often remarks on the outstanding results of her wit and charm."

"'Tis true, Charlotte," Alexander agreed. "Prinny holds a great fondness for Bella. He has said so several times in my hearing." Angling his head away from Charlotte, he winked at Bella, adding, "No one can credit his partiality for such a hoyden."

"I fail to see any wit or charm," Charlotte sniffed. "She will be barred from polite society, and Seventh Sea Shipping will follow suit."

"Pray, do not act like those stuffy women, Charlotte. You shall become old and boring long before your time." Bella could not resist the jibe. "The look on your face will bring on even more wrinkles."

Clearly afraid talk of wrinkles might turn into a brawl, Myron interceded. "I expect my business can withstand a bit of scandal. In fact, I know it can." Myron held Bella's arm tightly, running his thumb across the back of her hand. He said, though not loudly, "This is not the first time she has deservedly shown an aristo the rough side of her tongue, nor will it be the last, and I'm certain plain speaking causes no affront to God."

Nodding her head sharply in agreement, Bella turned her nose up at Charlotte in a childish pretense. Finally unable to contain his building mirth, Alexander started laughing aloud.

"I say, Holsworthy," he remarked with a grin, "you and your wife are just the fresh air we need at Court. It is so very dull listening to the same *on-dit* day after day. You'll ruin yourselves by morning, but it will liven things up nicely."

"I take back everything I said about missing you all this time," Charlotte declared, looking down her nose at her wayward cousin. "I had forgotten what a heathen you are."

"Then I shall endeavor to remind you as often as I can," Bella released a melodramatic harrumph. "There are more ladies headed our way. Shall I tell the story of the Gongulobibi priests revering me as a goddess?"

To keep reading go to your favorite book retailer.

SHIPMATE
A ROYAL REGARD PREQUEL NOVELLA

The heavy hands and sharp tongues of Bella Smithson's family have left her almost too timid to converse with a gentleman, much less conduct a husband hunt. Unfortunately, her overbearing aunt and managing cousin are determined to help her escape her black-hearted father and brothers.

Thanks to the Prince of Wales, retiring shipping magnate Myron Clewes has an ever-growing fortune, a fresh-minted peerage, a brand-new flagship, and an impossible set of requirements for a bride. Not least, she must be willing to leave England and everything she knows, possibly for good, in less than two months' time.

Bella's Happy-Ever-After in Royal Regard had its origins in a Happier-Than-She-Expected with her first husband, Baron Holsworthy, who gave her the confidence to steady her sea legs, take her life by the helm, and command her own voice, empowering a shy, young girl and unlikely adventurer to grow into one of King George IV's trusted advisors.

Continue on to the first chapter.

SHIPMATE

CHAPTER ONE

April 3, 1805
Bath, England

"There is Lady Lisbourne." Beneath the raucous dance music, Minerva, Lady Effingale, spoke in almost a full voice to emulate a whisper, making her niece wince beneath the likelihood of public humiliation. "I plan to introduce you, but best wait until she is alone; her eldest son's wife has a vicious tongue, and will not hesitate to call out your many faults."

Miss Isabella Smithson nodded, bottom lip caught between her teeth, fingers twisted in her skirt, knees shifting from side to side in her seat on the sofa between her aunt and cousin. Aunt Minerva's hard eyes, set deep in her forbidding face, roamed from Bella's hair, which must look a rat's nest by now, after an hour in a warm ballroom, to her hem, which had been splashed by a carriage in the street.

"Her fourth son is pockmarked, but not entirely without means, and if he won't have you, we might be able to place you with her as a companion. I'm told she is a bit dotty. And that gentleman there, in the blue waistcoat, is a widower."

Charlotte, the Marchioness of Firthley, leaned in, "He is a good-for-nothing, Mother, with six untamable children and an estate mortgaged to the hilt. You'll not tie my cousin to a man like that if I have anything to say about it." She patted Bella's arm, "And I do." Charlotte gently steered the subject to the relative cheapness of the decorations in the Bath assembly rooms, as opposed to London, a topic likely to occupy Lady Effingale for at least ten minutes.

For as long as Aunt Minerva was disparaging the environs, she could be relied upon not to criticize Bella. As soon as she reached the end of her complaints about the garish wallpaper, tasteless sculptures, and abundance of gold-trimmed mirrors, though, Aunt Minerva summed up with, "To think, I am reduced to social-izing in Bath, of all places. If Isabella had managed to keep her lemonade in her cup and not on the Duke of Lanceley's cravat, we would be in London, not a second-rate backwater. If only any gentleman there would look twice at you."

"Bath is hardly a backwater, Mother."

"It is hardly London."

Thankfully, Aunt Minerva didn't rake over Bella's encounter with the Duke of Lanceley. The very thought made her throat close. If only she could permanently close her ears against Lady Effingale's opinions of Bella's plain-as-pudding face, tree-stump-of-a-figure, stick-straight hair, drab-as-dirt disposition, designed-for-the-dustbin clothes, and havey-cavey father who provided a next-to-nothing dowry, then lost it in a gaming hell.

Every time Aunt Minerva said, *"my brother"* in that tone, Bella felt she was calling Satan out of Hell. No matter how often Char-lotte's father, Viscount Effingale, told Bella she was under his protection, it wasn't entirely true. Her father could remove her from the Effingale's manor house any time he chose, and he had done so by magistrate before. If Sir Jasper Smithson discovered any small advantage to having a plain, shy daughter who would never attract a man, the baronet would yank her back to Evercreech faster than a horse could throw a shoe, no matter who was paying the expenses for her husband hunt.

It wasn't as though Bella had asked to be brought out; she had begged to be left alone. She couldn't imagine a more horrid prospect than being forced to converse with unknown gentlemen on unknown topics amidst crowds of unknown aristocrats, with the end goal of being taken to wife by any man to make an offer. The thought of being alone with a new husband she had barely met made her stomach twist and mouth go dry. They had only been at the assembly a half-hour, and she already wished she were anywhere else.

Aunt Minerva had introduced Bella to every vaguely acceptable man in the room, excepting, of course, any who could find more attractive wives, and Bella would now be happy to excuse herself, with a headache beginning to pound behind her eyes.

When Aunt Minerva came out with, "...not remotely Incomparable, unless one had no other girl to compare with," Bella stood so quickly, she might have upset the chair, had her uncle not reached a hand out to steady her.

"If you will... er... retiring room. No, Charlotte, I will be perfectly fine alone."

When she reached the retiring room, she didn't even need to open the door to know it was filled with clacking hens. Bella could hear the *on dits* flying among too many women, even through the door. Instead of entering to discover herself another topic, she turned down a smaller hallway that surely must be servants' access to somewhere. No matter. Bella just needed a quiet place to rest her head and shut her eyes.

Standing in the unlit back hall, her head leaned against a wall, she hadn't even noticed the door open just a crack, about three feet away. Telling herself she was not, strictly speaking, a girl who would eavesdrop, she startled at, "...wallflower," and leaned closer.

She knew she had not put on a good showing tonight, but to be discussed and found wanting in the gentleman's study at the very first party was beyond the pale. Her face burned, and she shuffled closer to the wall, as though by proximity to the flocked wallpaper, she might become part of it.

"I take your point about wallflowers." The man's sardonic tone seeped through the door. "Low expectations, humility, and gratitude are all excellent qualities in a wife who will be forced to settle for an upstart baron who lives his life drifting between seaports."

He sounded worn down and tired, like Uncle Howard after one of Aunt Minerva's tantrums, but his voice was not resentful or angry, but kind, with a touch of humor.

"That's not what—"

"While I appreciate your effort to make His Royal Highness's commands more palatable, I am fairly certain he has no legal standing to make demands of a woman I marry, or require I remain in active service with my private fleet. I am past fifty years old, with a new barony and more money than I can spend in ten lifetimes. Surely he can understand my desire for a settled life and heir."

Bella tipped her head and moved just slightly to see if she could spot the man speaking, but without further opening the door and chancing discovery, there was no way. The second voice was not so kindly, masked slightly by the clinking of glassware and crystal. "Did you take your elevation as a reward, Holsworthy? For you might be better to view it as a bribe or a cudgel. The

Prince Regent wishes you on the high seas, not rusticating on a country estate, or he would not be adding ships to your fleet."

"His wishes are not lost on me, but I have made the prince and his father millions of pounds, and Seventh Sea Shipping will continue to pay out dividends until the next King George and I are both dust. Can that not be enough?"

"Not enough for the king, the regent, the Privy Council, most of Parliament, or the Foreign Office—not to mention your investors. You are the only one who thinks yourself unsuited as a diplomat. Do as your sovereign says, Holsworthy. Find yourself a seagoing baroness or board your new flagship without one."

Silence reigned for several long moments, until finally, the gentleman with the long-suffering tone said, "Clearly, the question of my living arrangements will not be solved today, but that is not to say I cannot seek out the future Lady Holsworthy, and your wife is waiting to begin the introductions. Shall we make good use of our proximity to the ballroom, where negotiations with appropriate young women can ensue? Perhaps if I find one amiable enough, she will talk the prince out of his new directive." He laughed. "I would gladly marry anyone who can change the regent's mind about anything."

Bella couldn't untangle the mumbling responses from the laughter, but could not miss the man chuckle and say, "Such a face! I will have you know, I find nothing objectionable about wallflowers."

To keep reading go to your favorite book retailer.